Praise for Tessa McWatt's THE SNOW LINE

'An exceptional, riveting read. Tessa McWatt's rare gifts never fail to enthrall me.'

Irenosen Okojie, author of *Butterfly Fish*

'Vivid, rich, and melodic. Layers of images, memories, and facts ask questions of connections, accountability, and desire—political and personal—and how we meet the complexities that make us. A beautiful read!'

Olumide Popoola, author of *When We Speak of Nothing*

'Tessa McWatt is one of our greatest living writers. *The Snow Line*, her new novel, is a profound meditation on love, ageing, and what it is to be a woman of mixed racial identity and culture. Profoundly moving and epic in its scope, this book provides us with wisdom and reckoning on today's world, one that is ecologically fragile and only just coping with a pandemic. Like all mature writers, McWatt's range of reference is vast and her depth of understanding of humanity plunges us into depths we all long to inhabit. She writes her characters with such intimacy we are thunderstruck by the book's final pages. I closed this book and shed tears.'

Monique Roffey, author of *The Mermaid of Black Conch*

'Tessa McWatt's writing is tender, unforgettable, utterly precise. Like performing surgery on a peach.'

Leone Ross, author of *This One Sky Day*

'A profound meditation on the music that strangers in a place can make together, and on how the music of a strange place can get inside us, and change us forever. I loved the journey the book takes us on, revisiting some of the geographies readers will remember from The Far Pavilions, while the echoes of King Lear provide an undercurrent of nature's aloofness, its potential for violence.'

Preti Taneja, author of *We That Are Young*

'Tessa McWatt's *The Snow Line* reveals life in overlapping panels: consciousness, memory, scenes of violence and of untenable beauty, 'everything dangerous enfolded into everything else.' Her prose has Michael Ondaatje's elliptical exactitude, Jane Gardam's terse confidence, but it accumulates, on behalf of her characters—a young woman and an old man, friends—a singular, lingering effect. *The Snow Line* is a small marvel.'

Padma Viswanathan, Scotiabank Giller Prize finalist for

The Ever After of Ashwin Rao

THE SNOW LINE

Also by Tessa McWatt

Out of My Skin
Dragons Cry
There's No Place Like . . .
This Body
Step Closer
Vital Signs
Higher Ed
Shame on Me: An Anatomy of Race and Belonging

TESSA McWATT

THE SNOW LINE

Random House Canada

PUBLISHED BY RANDOM HOUSE CANADA

www.penguinrandomhouse.ca

Library and Archives Canada Cataloguing in Publication

Title: The snow line / Tessa McWatt.
Names: McWatt, Tessa, author.
Identifiers: Canadiana (ebook) 20200348302 | Canadiana (print) 20200348299 |
ISBN 9781039000032 (EPUB) | ISBN 9781039000025 (softcover)
Classification: LCC PS8575.W37 S66 2021 | DDC C813/.54—dc23

Cover design: Lisa Jager
Cover image: Alex Harvey / Unsplash.com
Author photo: Christine Mofardin

Printed in Canada

10 9 8 7 6 5 4 3 2 1

Penguin
Random House
RANDOM HOUSE CANADA

For my brother and sister

'TIME PASSES TIME
does not pass. Time all
but passes. Time usually
passes. Time passing and
gazing. Time has no gaze
Time as perseverance.
Time as hunger.'

ANNE CARSON, *RED DOC* >

'In astronomy or planetary science, the frost line, also known as the snow line or ice line, is the particular distance in the solar nebula from the central protostar where it is cold enough for volatile compounds such as water, ammonia, methane, carbon dioxide, and carbon monoxide to condense into solid ice grains.'

WIKIPEDIA

Arrival

Four wedding guests disembark separately from the Dhauladhar Express at the Pathankot train station in the state of Punjab.

Yosh, the yoga teacher, arrives a day before the others, from Vancouver. He has come reluctantly, to work for tourists in the country he vowed to leave behind once and for all five years ago. His father is a millionaire in American dollars now, but many in India have not forgotten that his family was once deemed untouchable. He grips one wrist nervously.

Monica arrives from Toronto with maps and pink fingernails. She buys trinkets and garments — souvenirs to fill her spacious suitcase — ignoring her shrinking bank balance. She has not yet told her family the truth.

As Reema steps off the train onto the platform, she searches for her Indianness: something that might be bred in bone, or skin, or song, because she left this country before she could speak. The text messages from her Scottish boyfriend arrive with a dissonant ping in the Indian soundscape. She places a hand on her hip.

And then there is Jackson, knees brittle, a coin he has carried for fifty-four years tucked into his shirt pocket. As he sees Reema's hand fall from her hip towards her thigh, a crack splinters in his memory that lets dread through. Unknowingly Reema has brought with her a key that fits the door he had once locked tight. With only one task left to complete, he leaves the train station with strange whispers in his ear.

The stratosphere is dust and water, as well as particles — oxygen and nitrogen — so small that they are imperceptible. They make the sky blue. From here it's all one shade of blue. But there ... remember? There, all the colours seem separate, individual, the way the sky over the Himalayas has to stand back so as not to be pierced by the snow-capped peaks. Perhaps that trick of light is responsible for Jackson's blindness all those years — in fact for his whole life? And perhaps the slanted light accounts for Reema's fortitude.

No.

During those few weeks, snow and fire felt composed of the same chemical elements.

At a small train station in a town called Pathankot, four people with unrelated desires arrived for a wedding. Weddings are mirages; these four had no idea they would climb a mountain together and see different things from the top.

ONE

Jackson is as light as paper.

Here, on the lawn chair in the garden that looks out over the Maharana Pratap Sagar reservoir, he stares down at his legs and notices flakes of skin on his shins like moths in their final twitch. His once hairy, muscular calves are now scales on bone. He examines his socked feet in the leather sandals that Amelia told him never to wear with socks. Forgive him, Amelia.

Music rises in the distance. He glances towards the reservoir. The water is languid, the way it is on Long Pond lake, but this is a man-made body of water, hedged by mango and mulberry trees, not pine, not Massachusetts cedar.

He listens.

The wedding procession approaches, the music grows louder, and an echo bounces off the wall of the dam at the far reach of the reservoir. Jackson wipes his brow. He raises his hand to shield his eyes from the sun, and the dam winks at him. He knows the wizardry of hydroelectricity. He has been an engineer on projects like this on many rivers around the world, over decades in service to British and American engineering firms. But he has never before considered their acoustic drawbacks. He cups his hand over his ear as he stares down at his feet again, deciding he must release them from their cotton and leather cages.

Wicker chairs have been arranged on the lawn, and some guests are sheltering from the sun beneath the thatched roof veranda as they watch the revellers approach the compound's gates. Dancers make their way up the dirt road towards them. The crowd of extended family around him — women in blue, red, yellow saris, and men in embroidered sherwanis — clap their hands, and some whoop with excitement. Servers stand waiting, their uniforms crisp in the sun.

He raises his damp foot.

A horn bappaws, bells tinkle, cymbals shiver, and Jackson wipes sweat from his cheek, where there is the smell of jasmine. He slides his left foot out of the sandal and leans over in the chair, closer to the tree with heart-shaped leaves that make shade over his shoulder. He yanks at the sock to just come off, damn it. Patience, okay, Amelia. He peels, little by little, squinting as the sock reveals skin like casein on milk.

Dancers enter the garden, the women leading the band like conjurors come to rescue him. Tall, white English women — one who reminds him of his mother from a photo of her when she was young — are among the Indians, their arms flying as high as the baraat dancers, their rhythm no less precise. All of the women have bells on their ankles, tiny cymbals tied to their fingers. Their brocaded lehenga skirts hang heavy in the heat. Drummers beat their dhol faster than the horns can keep up with. The women stomp their feet.

Jackson examines his own foot, the fungus-yellowed toenails and the swollen, veined ankle. This ankle, for a man of eighty-six, is really not too bad. Another horn bappaws across the garden. He looks up to see the groom approaching on horseback behind the dancers. Jackson fixes his eyes on the bells at the women's ankles, tuning in to their pitch and to a high frequency vibration of the India he has known since he was a very young man, the India where he remains foreign. The horse snorts and shakes its head.

Amelia would never have let him wear the socks or go without a hat in Himachal Pradesh in March, but Amelia now watches from out there. Perhaps in the afterlife, toenails grow long, clear and unfungussed. Amelia is in the jasmine, the horse's tail, flicking small reminders to him: don't forget to wear your sunscreen, and never, ever, hork in front of the wedding guests, please, dear Jackson, because you'll embarrass me — we've known the bride's family for decades.

The dancers hop up and down, their hands in the air; the drums beat faster, a horn calls out, the recorded singing answers from a speaker positioned at the entrance to the garden, where a cement wall separates the retreat from the small village perched at the end of the peninsula. The horns blow in double time and more people jump. Up and down. He inhales. He is woozy with jet lag and droopy like the thin hanging pods of the laburnum across the garden. The shape of the leaves at his shoulder reminds him of sweets he missed as a boy when their family left England for Canada.

'I can hear the colour green,' I whisper to the boy next to me in the field with the others from our class. He pays me no attention. This Calgary boy is tall, and I know him only in my lies to my parents, who believe I have made my first friend in Canada. I repeat myself in case he hasn't heard — 'green, I hear green, isn't that …?' But the boy's friendship remains only the lie that saves face. I will never be popular, like my brother.

Jackson touches the leaf at his ear. Just come back, Amelia.

He picks the leaf and examines it.

Yesterday, as the bride, Jyoti, welcomed him to the garden and then took him on a tour of the retreat, she told him how grateful she was that her father's British friend, the owner, had let them use the place for the wedding. There was pride in her voice. Family and friends from Delhi, England, America and Kangra Valley were all gathered here for a week of festivities. Jyoti told Jackson that Vishnu hid under a tree like this to escape demons. Jackson declared it suitable for the shade he knew he'd need for the ceremony.

As they strolled in the garden, Jyoti pointed out flowers and views of the reservoir, but he was distracted by her hands, the swirls of dirt along the fingers and at her knuckles. He felt embarrassed for her, wondering how a bride could work in the garden the day before her wedding and greet guests with dirty hands. As she touched his arm and led him to meet her school friends from Delhi and her colleagues from London, he wondered if he should mention it, but then she introduced him to Reema, who had been her roommate at boarding school in London.

Between Reema and Jackson something thickened — a moment of recollection or apprehension, neither was sure which, because the something was without thought. He nodded as he reached out to shake hands. She took a step back while offering her own, her fingers clean, unlike Jyoti's. His mind flashed to a dark alleyway in Amritsar. She felt her throat tighten, like stage fright, while she examined the hairs that sprang from his ears and the way the skin of his chin hung nearly to his chest. Her green almond eyes, with lashes that nearly touched her strong brows, flickered before he quickly released her hand and glanced again at the ochre lines on Jyoti's fingers.

Reema could see how the henna on Jyoti's hands confused him. Pointing to it, she said, 'Isn't she a lucky bride?'

As the sun highlighted the diamond lines tucked into purls of henna, making swirls of eyes and droplets at Jyoti's wrists, Jackson — oh silly goat — remembered from nearly a lifetime of visits to India, that the more elaborate the henna pattern on the hands, and the deeper the colour of the mendhi, the more a groom loves his bride-to-be. He looked back at Reema, and his mind skipped again. There, in the place that had thickened, was the feeling of dread — *a rickshaw passes, there's the smell of sizzling oil.*

He turned in search of Deepak. 'Where's your father?' he asked Jyoti. 'I'd like to see him,' he said, and he walked away, Reema noting the bounce in his gait.

Now he rolls up the leaf in his hand and tosses it onto the lawn. The music is ever closer, and he feels it in his chest. Under Vishnu's tree he is safe, but Reema's face pained him. Young people pain him. They have everything and nothing. Jyoti, a descendant of this Kangra valley, with a degree in medicine from King's College in London, is a woman with everything to look forward to, but her friends seem to speak of nothing but mortgages.

He fumbles with his sock and drags it back over his foot. He sits back in the chair, but the sun has shifted, and he's now drenched in direct rays. He rises and shuffles towards the base of the tree. Until last year, the banks gave out mortgages to anyone off the street, paid young people to be in debt to them. Jyoti and her friends seem miffed that they missed the window for free money. Nothing is free, but for some reason these young people love debt.

Things are not the same, Amelia. His Boston house is mortgage-free, but it will never be home again.

Jackson will never be home in the US or even Canada, where his father transplanted the family from Liverpool in 1931 because oil was gushing in Turner Valley, Alberta. Home is not his parents' Liverpool, or the Niger Delta, where his father followed the oil when Jackson was ten. Nor is it Caracas or Nairobi, or Brunei or Brazil — none of the geysers his father taught him to run towards. Home has been a moving target throughout most of his life, and now, well, now …

1932 and Calgary is Imperial Oil is styrofoam snow is Chinook trees is mooning mountains is horn-cow rodeo and a wooden desk inkwell and Daisy Lewis's hair to her waist.

Jackson touches the trunk of Vishnu's tree, which is powdery and cool to his fingertips. He looks towards the entrance of the retreat and sees that the men are here. The groom has dismounted, sparing his horse the gravel path towards the pagoda that awaits them in the centre of the garden. A stable boy in a tattered uniform takes the reins of the animal and slowly brushes its flank, congratulating it for its performance. Jackson stares at the horse's fetlock, the ribbons tied there, the colossal weight of a beast on fragile joints.

To his left, beyond the garden wall, along the tree-lined road that runs on top of the dam, a large truck speeds towards the town of Talwara. The reservoir below is untouched by wind or turbulence. He once would have been attentive to the details of the dam — its structure, its inflow design, the sizing of the spillway and outlet works. But the business of hydraulic engineering does not interest him now.

Everyone is in place for the ceremony. The music stops. He moves from the tree to get a view. Glancing to his right he sees the jagged icing of the snow line on the Himalayas.

'Would you like me to move the chair into the shade,' says a thin voice to his left. Jackson turns and sees small dots of moisture on Reema's forehead. He wipes sweat from his neck. The woman is beautiful.

'I'm doing fine, thank you ... would you like it?' He pushes the chair towards her.

'No,' she says, 'I thought you ...'

'I'm not too bad for an old guy.'

She nods. Old white men must be pitied, she thinks, so she raises another smile for him. 'I'll fight you for it as the ceremony wears on,' she whispers. 'It's long.' She looks towards Aditya, the groom, who is climbing the steps to the platform where Jyoti stands in her red sari, a ruby-gold cradle of jewels around her neck, the pattern repeated at her forehead.

'Kanyadan is the first part of the ceremony,' Reema says, pointing towards Jyoti's father, who stands next to Jyoti.

Jackson takes in the pride on his friend Deepak's face. Jackson and Amelia have sent Deepak a Christmas card every year since 1988, when he and Deepak worked as consulting partners at the Bhakra Beas Management Board, Deepak a young man and Jackson nearing retirement. Twenty years of Christmas cards. Deepak lost his job last year in what everyone is now calling the biggest crisis since 1929 — *Jack, oh Jack, the banks failed and 2008 will go down in history*. Even hydroelectricity is not safe; even local dam projects can be ruined by lending money for nothing. Jackson shakes his head.

The world has become unsafe again, Amelia, as unsafe as it was in childhood. He stares out towards the reservoir beyond the meadow.

The hitch of the standpipe, the crank of a tin of corned beef, they're closing the dock, woman! 'Jackson get away from the window!' I am a little boy watching men in the street shouting for one another, their dirty fingernails, their gumboots torn. It's a general strike and all of Liverpool is a riot.

Reema watches the old man's chin, which shakes in thought. His jaw makes a chewing motion, side to side, like a cow's. Old white people make her nervous. They are purveyors of books and laws, of the ledgers of win and lose. They are smelly and bossy. If only she'd met her own white grandfather from California, who in photos had a Kirk Douglas dimple, she might have known better how to talk to this man. But she is not here for chit-chat.

She searches for someone else to befriend, but everyone else is coupled. Even Monica, Jyoti's Canadian cousin, her roommate for the week, is seated with a man. Jyoti's university and work friends, the Indian family Reema barely understands because of her basic grasp of Hindi — there is nowhere to escape, and she knows the ceremony will be tedious. Her brother's traditional Indian wedding was a circus of wanna-be-more-than-half-Indian shenanigans, even though he had married an English woman. In their family, their mother secretly kept small traditions of Diwali and Holi with candlelight and colour, but her brother had long dreamed of displaying his internationalism, going the whole hog with a wedding that was even more elaborate than this one.

Hell, what else is there to do: she drags the chair into the shade beside Jackson. She leans towards him. 'He is asking Aditya not to fail his daughter,' she says softly, explaining what Deepak is doing on the platform with the bride and groom, 'not to fail in his pursuit of dharma … artha … kama …' she whispers, and suddenly sits down on the chair herself, light-headed. Aditya answers Jyoti's father with what sounds like a promise, and then repeats it three times.

Jackson glances at Reema from time to time during the next phase of the ceremony. Her eyes shut tight? The massaging of her thumb? He can't ask for the chair back now. He moves closer to the platform, braving the sun, taking up a position near a pond with pink and white lotus flowers choked together, brooding in the heat. The pond is surrounded by a few vacant garden chairs that he keeps an eye on.

Aditya lights a fire in the centre of the pagoda.

Aditya and Jyoti sit. He recites a verse, then she answers, as they hold hands. Jackson knows these words — not the Sanskrit, he is useless at languages. He knows their intonations. Knows the sound of impossible promises. Fifty-seven years of marriage brings knowledge that words alone cannot. He turns back to look for Reema.

She has her face in her hand, elbow on her knee. Her arms are long and shapely. The feeling of being on the edge of a dark shadow hits him again and he touches his forehead. What has he forgotten?

In Boston his house is shut up, newspapers cancelled, neighbours either side alerted to the fact that he will be away for at least a fortnight, his ticket flexible, the invitation open. These long-time friends have made it possible for him to escape the dragging on and on of chilly weather by giving him the honour of attending the wedding of their daughter. There's nothing he needs in that house, so what is nagging him?

The groom leads the bride around the platform, slowly, reciting the first four steps. This part of the ceremony Jackson enjoys. He and Amelia have been to a few Hindu weddings in their day — families of the friends he made as far back as 1948, during his first-ever internship in the Punjab province: the engineers, the management, even the accountant from Amritsar. There is something he needs to remember. He looks back at Reema and tries to find it. His thoughts slip beneath the present like tectonic plates, but he pulls himself back to the ceremony.

Jyoti is reciting as they circle the fire. Her sari is tied to Aditya's sherwani, and now she is leading him. They are taking these seven steps, she is saying. As they walk around the flame, there are pledges made between bride and groom that Jackson knows in his solar plexus, which he touches now.

'We have taken the Seven Steps. You have become mine forever. Yes, we have become partners. I have become yours. Hereafter, I cannot live without you. Do not live without me. Let us share the joys. We are word and meaning, united. You are thought and I am sound. May the night be honey-sweet for us. May the morning be honey-sweet for us. May the earth be honey-sweet for us. May the heavens be honey-sweet for us. May the plants be honey-sweet for us. May the sun be all honey for us. May the cows yield us honey-sweet milk. As the heavens are stable, as the earth is stable, as the mountains are stable, as the whole universe is stable, so may our union be permanently settled.'

———

'Are you musical?' says Reema behind Jackson, which disrupts his trance and makes him wonder how long he has been standing staring at the vacated pagoda. He looks about the garden and sees Jyoti and Aditya greeting the friends and relatives gathered around the wishing tree.

'Why do you ask?' Jackson adjusts the shirt collar beneath his suit jacket, feels the wetness there, oh god it's hot, Amelia. He does not want to talk to anyone.

Reema tries not to stare at everything that is old about him — his lizard neck, the gaps between his gums and his teeth, the liver spots on his hands — but there is a mole below his ear with a single white hair growing out of it like a spike. She keeps coming back to it as though it might be magic and she can wish on it. 'I've been asked to lead a group for tomorrow evening. We will sing a classical canon, or at least make it sound like one — it's just three words,' she says. Of course, it's nonsense that Jyoti should ask her to make her guests sing classical western music in India, but she is trying to do her part and not be annoyed at the Europeanness she thought she was leaving behind on this trip.

'You sing,' he says flatly, almost as an accusation. He fidgets, moves side to side, one foot, then the other, as though about to run.

'Have you added your wish?' he asks, to loosen the air between them. He points to the lemon tree that has been covered in paper tags, tied there by guests offering wishes to the married couple. 'I wished for them to stay awake to each other,' he says. You'd be proud, Amelia.

She turns towards the lemon tree to see the newlyweds reading the scraps of paper, with laughter and appreciative 'aaww's. The old man's wish is odd, but whatever he meant by it, the sentiment is kinder than her own. 'I wished for them to see one another in the mirror when they look at themselves — there is a Hindi saying like this,' Reema says. But a mirror is a trick, she thinks, and smiles.

When her eyes flash at him he feels it again, something unnerving.

Amritsar, young male bodies, white kurtas, approaching a woman, their arms like elephant trunks, trumpeting, teeth bared and laughter like ice.

He clears his throat.

'Come and hear us tomorrow. Or join us,' she says, making an unnecessary effort out of habit.

Florida, he thinks.

'Florida,' he had said to Amelia a decade ago as he held out brochures for bungalows in gated communities. 'Florida for half the year, then back here for the summers.' His plans were a surprise he'd kept for a dark day in late January when the temperature in Boston dipped to −9 degrees Fahrenheit. 'In Marlin Bay, now, it's over 70.' Amelia had looked up at him from her Opera Guild magazine with less than curiosity. Curiosity would have been at least a step towards him. Her look was to the side of him, to something she always saw when he did something wrong. She took the brochures and opened them, taking her time, greeting the images with a smile. Across the slow turn of each page it gradually dawned on him that there was probably very little opera in the Florida Keys, and if they went south in winter she'd miss the whole season at the Boston Opera House. As the moment of waiting for her response grew longer, he thought of her days — full, busy days — which included leading a chapter of Girl Guides, representing them at international conferences;

being a classroom assistant at two local elementary schools, helping with reading and music in the afternoons; supporting their local education trustee during elections. The moment of waiting dragged on for an eternity.

'My wife ...' he says to Reema, and his hand moves to his breast pocket, then his trouser pockets, front and back, the feeling of having misplaced her. 'So many places to live in ... so many ... but ...' Now he's gone too far and must not give anything away to a young woman he cannot trust. He scrambles to think of something that will deflect the mood and change the subject. When he has it, his chest rises, nearly a heave of laughter, and he says, 'but so few places to get a pedicure.' He holds a straight face, waiting, then chuckles.

She laughs, and a tiny opening appears for sympathy.

TWO

The only external sound is the whir of the fan above his bed, but inside him is a high-pitched rushing noise. He turns over on his side to listen. The wedding guests are asleep, but Jackson's arteries are demanding his attention.

The guests span the ages, but he is the oldest. They have come from Delhi, Mumbai, London, and even North America, because the bride and groom are modern, wealthy and, he guesses, people who are hoping to maintain the status quo in next month's Indian general election, rather than BJP voters. One of the young men, long hair to his shoulders, is different, out of place as he stands back and watches the others gather in a constant cocktail party.

'Advani has the best ears,' one guest in a sparkling sherwani, holding a small glass of liqueur, had said to a circle of men discussing political candidates after dinner. 'He has the ears of Russia and America, one each side.' The others laughed approvingly. 'Too much fuss about politics at the moment,' another said, and set off grumblings among a few who appeared to become old before Jackson's eyes. One declared that he admired the Gujarat model of development. Others nodded. Congress supporters, their lives are comfortable, no reason to tip the scales further right to the BJP. Jackson knows they are the sort of young men that India is breeding now — who speak of mortgages, call centres and start-ups, of short holidays in hill stations. When he'd lived here long ago, he thought he'd slowly begun to understand the culture — or at least the dominant culture — to see how gods and labour and animals were drawn together in paintings. Gods and labour and animals were the triumvirate, not unlike Brahma, Vishnu and Shiva. And each had its place in the life of ordinary Hindus. Gods for stories, labour for good living, animals to worship. He thought he could make sense of things if he looked at them through this lens. But these new men are a puzzle.

The guests danced. They drank. They sang. Jackson watched in amazement.

I sit on my mother's lap at the piano and want her to teach me how to do the things she does with her fingers and to make the ... is this jazz? It is as new as snow and pancakes and mean boys. She pushes my fingers down on the keys — 'Like this, Jackson,' she says — and oh, my, this is something, and this is a feeling I want to keep.

Reema left him alone for most of the evening, thankfully. She is a young woman unaware of the force of her beauty, and he does not understand what it is about her that shames him. At the end of the night she accompanied him to his room. When she took his arm, he shook her off, but, Amelia, forgive him, he didn't mean to offend.

As they reached his door, he told her that he knew very little about music; it was his wife who sang. Reema cocked her head at him like a sparrow at a whistle. She said maybe his wife would like it if he joined their group on Friday.

But what is there to like or to join at this point? He has recurring images of Indian rituals long outmoded. Sati was criminalised long ago, but his desire is for sati in reverse: when he scatters Amelia's ashes, he will scatter himself too, throw himself upon them and dissolve in a pile of bone on bone, precious and disappeared.

He turns over and switches on the bedside lamp. A quick glance to check on the tea canister perched on his suitcase. He scrutinises the room, decorated to high standards, with a mix of European and Indian furnishings, and North Indian tapestries and carvings on the wall.

The owner of this retreat is a man whom Jackson envies. A good thirty years younger than he is, Mike is the kind of man with the courage to irrigate and plant, to fight off snakes and scorpions, to grow food, to build shade and make a patch of dry valley so beautiful that a couple's future could be launched here, two families joined. Later in the spring Mike will hold retreats for yoga groups from the States and Britain. With the help of people from the local settlements and drivers from Amritsar, whom he pays higher than the going rate, he organises the food and the outings that allow guests to feel like they have escaped the west. Mike is a bachelor, a man for many not one, and this is the one thing about him that Jackson does not envy.

After his first job in the Punjab ended in 1948, Jackson had wanted to stay on, even though the English had left, even though there was war over Kashmir. He was his own man, making his way without his parents or his brother, and he had wanted to make his mark. But he would soon have a wife, would have to be responsible. His father had moved the family around the world for oil, and Jackson would end up moving Amelia around the world for water; he would be a hydraulic engineer who would never plant anything in soil.

A sudden, dense thud lands on his roof. As sure as night it's a body. Then a second, along with snarling and growling. The roof will collapse with the brawling of beasts on top of it. Jackson rises quickly, hand on his back to straighten up, and stares up at the ceiling. Good Lord in heaven. He hears doors open and slam in the room beside his, and a man shouting across the garden. Jackson stands still, concentrating on the tea canister as he follows the sounds. The man's shouts get closer and there's the sound of wood thunking above. The bodies tumble off and onto the gravel below. There's dragging and scuffling, more growling, shouting. Then suddenly a lull.

At last the only sound in the room is the fan. He walks to the tea canister, picks it up, and oh, Amelia, you wouldn't have been frightened, not you.

But it's a new decade, why won't you dance, she whispers to me, swaying, her hair all perfume and puff, the Andrews Sisters loud and out of step in Brunei, on the lawn of a friend of the Sultan's, me with my hands in pockets, frowning, her mother and father watching from the far corner, no clue that the 1950s would bring a wedding but no babies, no matter how hard we tried, no babies.

THREE

He wakes to the sound of women's voices and a swishing broom across the tiles outside his door. The tea canister is there on top of the suitcase, but on its side, idiot, be more careful. Particles of Amelia must still be on their kitchen counter where he transferred her from the urn to the canister for easier carriage. He rises, presses his thumb into his lower back and sets it upright again, then coaxes his legs to the bathroom.

Dressed and shaven, a tiny nick near his chin, he makes his way onto the veranda and down the short set of stairs. He notices smatterings of blood that the women have missed in their cleaning. There is more along the tiles, the railing, a splash on the lemon blossoms. He takes careful steps, respectful of those growls in the night. His knee clicks, but he presses on. On the pebbles at the bottom of the stairs, more blood and something that looks like liver.

'Civet cat,' the owner tells him at breakfast, placing a chair beside Jackson's and sitting down to explain the disturbance in the night. Jackson feels included in a secret in the way other guests have not been; he doesn't need protecting, and Mike has sensed this. He sits tall, waiting for the slow yarn, the way stories are drawn out in this part of the world, the way events become parables all their own. As a young man in the Punjab, Jackson watched as dogs gorged on a sambar fawn in Choti Badi Nagal village, only to hear of leopards eating the dogs a few weeks later, the villagers understanding something he could not about nature's providence.

'One bit the head off the other,' Mike says, 'and we found the head down the dirt path this morning. Oddest-looking things — have you ever seen one?'

'Not in the flesh, but, yes … part raccoon, hyena, cat … ugly.'

'Not ugly,' Mike says flatly. Jackson's heart sinks. Mike leaves to supervise the serving of more omelettes to Jyoti's hungry relatives. Jackson finishes his tea.

Others start to push away dishes, brush crumbs from their laps, rise to excuse themselves from the tables. Among them, the young man with long hair who stood apart at the reception calls for the others to meet at the gate for their walk to the meadow. Jackson has reservations about joining them. The groom's parents head towards the gate, along with aunts, cousins, and young people from abroad who remind Jackson of children at camp ready for a game.

It's hot as hell already, the hottest day yet of the five he's been in India. He has thinner socks on today, in canvas shoes that are good for walking. He must not hesitate; he must find the right place to deal with the contents of the canister. The reservoir is part of the Beas River; the water will eventually flow north as it divides Amritsar from Kapurthala, into the Punjab where he and Amelia once lived. She might like to travel back. He checks in with his feet: fine. His back hurts; the bed was hard. But everything else is as strong as it was on the last walk he took with her in Boston, yellow leaves at their feet, autumn air like a slap, and Amelia nearly racing him home, laughing. Friends have always remarked on his fitness. In the last six months they've looked at him differently, their faces telling him the obvious — that he's less without her.

He checks in with his bladder.

'Cross the peninsula at the dead cow,' Mike says to the college friends who are dressed like real hikers. This whole thing is a bad idea, Jackson thinks as he turns, checking to see if Reema is among the others. She stands near the gate, spots him, and waves.

He hesitates.

'Going slow?' he says as he walks towards her.

'Of course,' Reema says, opening the gate for him.

He lets a young guest in flip-flops go ahead of him, then follows.

'In my day they called those thongs,' he says to Reema, pointing at the young man's feet, 'but these days I'd get a look if I said I used to wear them.'

He begins to trust her when she smiles. A woman's opinion would help. Women know what other women want. Amelia never talked about these things with him. When he brought up topics like funerals and a future without him, sure that he would be the first to go, she changed the subject, and she refused to mention her own wishes. By the time he really needed to know, she could only blink, her left eye drooped shut, and her brain locked away.

He heads down the path.

'You're in good nick,' Reema says loudly to his back, enjoying the old man's safari outfit and the way he pumps his arms like a speed walker. He holds back a dry branch of a eucalyptus tree that crosses the path, waiting for her to clear it. She feels a desire to pat him on his shoulder, the way you pat horses or large dogs.

'I *was*,' he says, and there's his bladder, right there, a little nudge. Never mind. He keeps his eyes on his feet, making sure not to trip. There are small red flowers on dry bushes along the path and he begins to enjoy himself, pleased by the word 'nick', which reminds him of the Englishness of his family gone so long ago, displaced by North American plain speaking. 'Have you been here before?' he asks her.

The path opens out to a meadow and the reservoir. At the far reaches of the water, the Pong Dam stands as steady as a temple. To use a river to build a nation, yes, he thinks — this is the height of expertise, progress. And freedom.

'Not me, no. Part of my family is from here,' she says as she comes up beside him and they stop.

'Your accent is very English.'

'*Accha*,' she says, trying to prove some local pedigree, but she's a fake, not funny even to herself, saying this word over and over in her mind since she arrived, but feeling stripped of her claim to it with every day that passes. Her Indianness is fractured and bruised, but this is not something to share with this old man. As Jyoti's oldest friend, she had helped with the guest list at the final stage: cutting the unnecessaries; the bride-to-be insisted that her father's long-time mentor in hydroelectricity should not be left out, particularly because he'd just lost his wife. But both Reema and Jyoti resented that a single person would occupy a room meant for two. 'My parents moved to London when I was a baby,' she says.

He can smell rose water or hyacinth or something in her perfume that makes an old man feel like living. If Reema suggests this lake as the ideal spot, he'll do it. He's considered taking Amelia back to that garden in Brunei, where he proposed to her, or to the basin of the Rio Chagres in Panama, where she would sit, hour after hour, painting watercolours of the rocks at the eddy of a tiny waterfall while he surveyed the banks of the river with his colleagues. But if Reema says, Jackson, this is perfect, this still water, these migrating birds to visit daily, he'll do it. A woman would know.

'Do you like London?' he says.

'Mostly, yes. Do you like Boston?' She touches the back of her neck where a fly escapes her fingers. Even with this small talk she'd rather talk to an old man who has lived a life than to Jyoti and her mates who are pretending to live theirs. Surely, though, it's not as simple as liking a place. Everything inside her is shifting and it might not matter where she eventually finds herself. *Accha*, she thinks, and holds on to the sound.

Jackson tries to gauge the exact colour of her eyes. Previously they were green, but now they might be brown and, Amelia, young people can change right before you in an instant. 'It's hard to move around so much. Boston is where we ended up, by chance,' he says. The air on the meadow opens itself up to him. He inhales. Insects circle his head. To the left there is a buzzing mass of flies preying on the carcass of a calf, fallen between the rocks, rotting, the mouth eaten away first, its grin ghoulish.

'By chance?' She sighs and shifts her weight. *By chance, with any luck, in the scheme of things, under the circumstances*: what do these mean when all along, every step of every day, there's a choice to go left, to go right, to backtrack, to run, to hide. Until this week, or perhaps even this moment, she had believed in the idea that things merely unfold. But unfolding is an illusion. Real choice is fast as a straight clean blade.

To the right of the meadow there are gullies where the water is low and lapping at sandy ridges. She rests her hands on her hips again, noticing she's doing this a lot, and at the same time noticing a man looking at her. The yoga teacher — tall, dark, his long hair pushed behind his ear. She turns quickly back to Jackson.

'My father's father was English, and his mother was Goan. They lived in America and weren't very Indian at all. My father became a musician, left the States and moved to India. He married my mother, whose family had land in this valley, not *by chance*,' she stresses, and sees that the old man doesn't flinch at her sarcasm. 'He was determined to be Indian.' But she doesn't say that he ultimately failed. Events are not accidents. People make decisions: to stay, to leave. Reema has made the effort to be at this wedding in order to visit the valley where her mother's mother grew up, and to give herself time to think.

Jyoti is lucky. She is simply Indian. Her grandfather was not English, her father was not born in America. For Jyoti this valley is a playground, an extension of Delhi life. In London when Jyoti is called a Paki, she does not have to hate one part of herself that is abusing the other part.

Reema looks towards the shore where the others are gathering. A small wooden boat putters towards them. A valley of drowned stories, her mother calls it, where there are only monkeys and lost fables. Her mother has never spoken well of this valley, rescued from it as she was by Reema's grandfather's status in trade. She was given a place in a state college in Delhi that had been developed to train women in accounting and business management. And later she was rescued again by defying the arrangement her parents had made for her marriage. When she fell in love with Reema's father, they eloped, ensuring that her valley days had ended.

'What did you do for a living?' she asks Jackson, remembering to be polite, but knowing the answer and so only indulging him.

'I was a hydroelectric engineer,' he says.

'Yes, now I remember,' she says, and turns, walking again to catch up with the others. 'Not by chance, though,' she adds. Old people speak of job titles and salaries and what is supposed to happen in life like they have a special map to follow.

'I say the wrong things,' Jackson mutters behind her. He will not be taken for an ignorant old geezer who thinks that civet cats are ugly.

She stops, looks back at him apologetically; she has been taught never to disrespect elders. 'I'm sorry. I didn't mean to cut you short,' she says. The running back and forth inside, the butting up against herself, continues. She touches his arm and leads him towards the others. 'How are you doing? Hot?'

'How do you know what I did for work?'

'Jyoti told me.' She holds his arm tighter in hers to comfort him.

He likes the thought that he has been spoken about for his work. There is little left to feel proud of, and no one to inherit the pitiful retirement income he managed to secure. 'And why did she tell you?'

Daddy is painting the backyard fence as I hold the tin into which he dips his brush. I notice how the white paint globs at the joints of the timber. He is not a painter, I tell myself. He has skills no one can see, his talent under the big words I do not understand, his magic in his fingers when they fan through the dollar bills he gives the paper boy.

Reema decides to spare the old man Jyoti's unkind thoughts about her father's American power dam partners.

'You know,' she says, pointing to the dam as she continues to walk. She sees a few of the other guests now swimming, and the yoga teacher standing, watching the expanse of the water beyond the peninsula. 'In the '60s they moved out thousands of people and flooded a hundred villages in the valley in order to make this reservoir.' She turns to register his reaction. Her father told her this casually when she was a child, unearthing a family story and instantly embedding it in a mind too young to cope with it.

'These things are difficult,' Jackson says. You can't stop progress, can't keep an entire province in the dark when opportunities come along, can you?

'Difficult?'

Jackson tries to get his breath. She is young, he reminds himself. 'It's necessary for irrigation. Where did your family move to, then?'

'My mother's parents were *ousted*,' she says. *Ousted* is her father's term, which he uses only when speaking to other Indians. It's the word the valley's petitioners use in the courts, in the newspapers, with new lawyers every year. She wants to write it into the clay at the shore.

Beyond the peninsula, three freight trucks trundle across the bridge on their way to Talwara, and the sun's reflection from their steel panels dazzle like a pinwheel movie. Jackson shields his eyes with his hand. The swimming guests call out for the stragglers to jump in, join them. Curious local villagers watch the party from the incline above the lake. Jackson and Reema retreat to their own thoughts — he, remembering the word *murabbas* for the acres of land that the Indian government gave to people displaced by hydroelectric projects; and she to dwell on photographs sent to her by her father.

So many drowned stories. Her father had chased music from California to Chennai, where he tried to be more Indian than the

Mahatma, but he turned against the country when Reema was only a year old. Ever since, he has been like a chief detective for the prosecution, uncovering clues that will explain to his family why he uprooted them. He clips out articles, photos, and sends them to her in the post, despite the fact that she lives only miles from his home. One of the images from many years ago is of a roof of a village house jutting a foot above water in a valley just like this one, which had been flooded for irrigation. The other is of parched, cracked soil like a crater on a dead planet. The images don't connect to anything in her experience, and she doesn't know what her father is trying to tell her.

There are secrets in dust, too. The owner of the retreat told her that thirty thousand families were displaced from this valley; only those who had owned land here were given land elsewhere. Reema's family doesn't fit into a single story. *Accha*.

They have nearly arrived at the shore, close to where the yoga teacher stands. Jyoti's brother, now swimming, waves to them — *come on in, the water's perfect*. Reema waves back. Jackson surveys the peninsula with a hand cupped to shade his brow.

'Things aren't in our control,' Jackson says.

Reema takes a deep breath, holds it and her tongue, lets the breath out slowly.

Jackson feels the sun on his forehead, smells the rotting dead calf: there it is again, the feeling of something to be wary of with this young woman.

In the silence she reminds herself that she has no old people in her life, not like the other women here, not like Indian families with layers and layers of relatives across generations. 'You should come at least to listen to the choir,' she says.

Jackson has a thought. He turns and heads back over the meadow towards the bloated carcass, to the path that will take him back up to the retreat, to his room beside the lemon tree, where he'll retrieve the canister, then hire a driver to take him to Varanasi, where he'll pour Amelia into the Ganges. This is his best idea yet. It was described for him clearly, all those years ago when he worked in the Punjab. The male seed develops into bones, the female blood results in flesh. At the end of life, a reversal takes place in the heat of cremation and divides flesh from bone. The spirit is released. Ashes scattered into the holy river will ensure rebirth. He shuffles across the meadow, careful to avoid the piles of cow shit along the way, aware that the cormorants are flying in formation, low like paper planes over grass.

Don't hesitate, Jackson.

The cormorants cry, human voices from the lake become polyphonic and irritating, and his shirt is soaked. Then there's a flash to his left and small stalls appear — with fruit, shoes, rows of pinnis, balushahis and gur ka halwa, cauldrons of frying samosas. A rickshaw passes him and he is squeezed out of the road into an alley near the Golden Temple where the men in white kurtas surround the woman. She is wearing a headscarf; they are tall, short, fat, thin, all manner of Hindu men and not one of them notices him, standing, staring, stunned as they jeer at her, push her, peel away her scarf, barricade her with their legs, their penises making tents in their kurtas … and, oh, the cry of cormorants …

'Jackson!'

When he opens his eyes, he smells cow shit.

'It's fine, it's fine, they've gone to get help,' Reema says and he realises that his head is resting on her lap. One of her hands is on his chest, the other on his forehead. The clouds above break apart and scatter.

'I'm okay. I am. I'll take her to the Ganges,' he says.

'Better if you stay here with me. Help is coming.'

The groom's friend stands over him now and cold lake water drips onto Jackson's arm. Someone else is dripping water onto his leg. They say death comes to your left side and if it's time ... oh Amelia, isn't it funny to be young, on a picnic, swimming in a lake, making fun of old people. Never mind.

'She loved to sing,' he says, looking up at Reema. The young woman's eyes are not cold, and he relaxes into them. He will ask her; he must do the right thing with the tea canister. Why didn't he dance with Amelia on that New Year's Eve in Brunei? 'I doubt I'd be any benefit to your choir,' he says.

Reema presses gently on his forehead. 'I'm sure that's not true.'

When he looks to his left the dripping friend is gone; others surround him. The retreat owner arrives, and asks them to stand back.

'Clever move to get a beautiful woman's attention,' Mike says. 'I should try that one!' Mike smells of fish as he bends to take Jackson's wrist, feeling his pulse.

'A few tricks left in the old guy yet,' Jackson says, and with Mike's help he sits up, catching sight of his soaked trouser leg where his bladder has let loose.

Four

Their red backsides are hairless, rough, as though they've dragged them along the pink stones beside the lake. Three adults, two babies. Reema stops and holds her breath. She steps forward as the mother flips the baby off her back and licks its red raw bottom. Reema's stomach churns. The monkeys scamper up into the forest beyond the pebbled trail, frightened by her footfalls. Ha! They cannot know how slight a threat she is. She treads more softly. *Accha*. Come little monkey, come here, there is nothing to be frightened of. She is not a poacher; she does not want the pittance the Indian government offers to deliver you up, to sterilise you, little monkey. She wants only a moment without humans.

The heat is easing, the sky reddening over the wall of the dam, and oh what a thing it is to strangle a river to make a lake. She stops again as cormorants in formation hold tight to their V above her. Farther along to her right on the meadow, the dead calf's legs are bent towards the sky. She moves over the grass and stones along the peninsula towards the widest expanse of the reservoir, at the mouth of the dam.

The monkeys were hiding this morning, when the wedding guests took their dip, making noise, frolicking the way wedding guests are scripted to for the sake of the bride and groom, as though life is simple. Life is simple only for monkeys. This peninsula of jungle, meadow, shore is theirs again: some of the guests have driven across the tree-lined bridge to visit Talwara; others are doing yoga with the long-haired man with camel eyes.

Reema is sorry to have disturbed the bare-naked macaques. When her mother's family lived in this valley, the farmers killed the monkeys that destroyed their crops. Now, even with the bounty to limit their numbers, monkeys are as sacred as cows, and in Shimla the authorities have erected a new statue of Hanuman. Out of the jungle, onto the meadows, into the streets of the village. *Accha.*

She takes a deep breath. She must be more *haa*, what? Gentle. In her thoughts. To cows, to monkeys, yes, okay, but also to people like Jyoti, the placid Monica who shares her room, and to the old man who has lost his wife. She must not resent so much. Weddings bring this on. At her brother's she drank until hell was in her throat. She stood small before her tall father — famous in his family for his hot temper — and she threw her head back, pointed her finger at his heart, and told him she would quit music college in London, move to America and become a lesbian: his worst nightmares in one sentence, designed to loosen the harness of his expectations.

She reaches the flat shoreline. The water is low, wetting only the base of the larger stones. They are bold, more colourful than the stones on the path, and there are no monkeys in sight. She will try harder for gentleness. She touches her stomach.

When Robert said *We will be happy,* her insides somersaulted; she had to sit down. A house with blunt, orange angles formed in her mind.

There is still time to consider everything, still two weeks within the safe limit. Still something that she must see the way her mother saw that antelope.

The family myth of Reema's birth is that she was named for the white antelope that sent her mother into labour twenty-six years ago. But there are no antelope in Delhi. Her mother is a fantasist, which is one way to survive her marriage to the Anglo-Indian-who-will-not-listen. The man who wore American then Indian then British the way people wear clothes. Cloth covers skin differently with each fabric. But, still, it covers. When her father's romance with tea and Hinduism failed, he moved on to England. 'Stranded, we're stranded on an island,' he says now as he clips items from Indian newspapers to send without comment to his daughter. The latest came just before she left for this wedding. A small brown envelope contained a clipping from the *Kochi Times*, one of the many Indian newspapers he scours regularly, reporting the story of a young woman travelling on a train in Kerala when a man had tried to rob her. He smashed her head on the carriage wall and threw her out of the train. He jumped out after her, found her and carried her to the woods near the track and raped her. A few days later she died of her injuries.

A family full of fear and uncertainty needs its own myth, and so the antelope is theirs.

She climbs over a pile of pink and white conglomerates, marking the distance between herself and the retreat, out of sight of anyone who might be watching from the lookout. Her ankles twist and turn; her sandals slip. Down here she will be able to do as she has wanted for days. She looks around, sees no one close, fishermen in the distance. Her voice is strong because she has been learning the shuddha swaras from her new teacher in London. She has the power to scare the fish from their nets. Oh fishes and frogs and salamanders, do not fret.

After ten years of English choral singing and the training in western classical music that her father encouraged her to take up as a child, Reema is finally learning Indian notes. Sadhana, recommended by a college tutor as the best swaras teacher in London, has been teaching Reema sounds that have been lost from her family since her father rejected India. *Taka da da da da, takada daa, takada, da.* Sounds from inside her.

Sadhana has told her that the swaras originate in animals and each corresponds to a specific place in the body. If she sings *sa* she is a peacock; *ni* and she will be an elephant. *Re* is the bull, and for this the sounds will rise from between her legs. She looks towards the lake; perhaps the fishermen will mind. She walks on, further around the peninsula, to be out of earshot.

There are two figures seated on the precipice that hangs out over the water. Lovers. Another effect of weddings. But this precipice is a lie, young man, young woman. It is not real rock. Nothing here is as it seems. The lake is a flooded river, these cliffs are earth, sand, not solid; each year when the monsoons come, they crumble like fudge sliced by a knife. Your homes on the hill will one day be drowned.

Her mobile buzzes; she takes it from her pocket. Robert wants to know how she is, whether she is feeling better. She tucks the phone back in her shorts and continues on, moving higher up, closer to the forest, where there are fewer stones, and walking is easier.

Tiny wildflowers are lined with red veins, throbbing with spring. Her great-great-grandmother might have walked just here, might have squatted over there, might have entered the forest by that path to gather dry branches. At the end of the day she would have followed the cows slowly up the path, pacing patiently behind them as they lumbered and the sky darkened, then at home she would have built a fire with the branches and placed pots on top of it. Gather, build, eat, sleep. Is such a simple day really possible? Reema stops and stands with her legs apart. She squats, trying to keep her heels on the ground the way she has seen yogis do, the stance the wedding guests wobbled into and tumbled out of as she watched this morning's yoga class. She loses her balance. No Londoner squats. She tries again. Please, someone teach her how to squat and get up again, to trace planets in motion, to redistribute wealth. But also to be free. Free to do nothing.

'You must find a man who is willing to eat kuchala for your love,' her mother said when Reema was a girl. Her mother was referring to a distant cousin from Kangra who fell in love with a young man from her own village. The couple's parents disapproved, would not allow them to marry. A marriage was soon arranged for the girl with a man from a hill village near Dharamsala. The day before the wedding was to take place, the two lovers met again and the young man told his beloved that he refused to live without her, that he had already swallowed berries from the strychnine tree, *kuchala*, and please, here, as he held out berries in his palm, would she join him in a suicide pact? The distant cousin turned and ran, her ears pounding with doubt, to the young man's parents. While her arranged wedding took place in the Himalayan village, the Kangra boy lay convulsing in hospital, his lips foaming, abandoned. There is a saying in their village that the strongest love is from a man who would even eat kuchala for it.

Reema stands up and moves on. A bird in the trees to her left has a call that is nearly a full sentence. *Sweet lean wing-sister*, it might be saying. She stops, gazes at the lake, then down at the ants marching one by one in a circle around the red flowers.

Robert's voice is deep and growly. On a Monday evening in a small Covent Garden pub occupied only by Robert and his two friends at the bar and Reema and her two friends at a corner table, all the voices were distinct. *'Don't be ridiculous.'* Those first words she heard from him were stern, but when she turned, she saw that his face and voice didn't match. His face was feminine and soft. She had learned early on from her English friends at school, and later at Trinity Laban College, that English men with soft voices — those who had been to public school and had learned how to subdue themselves — were the ones she should fancy. But Robert was Scottish, worked as a copywriter, and wore suits that were a fraction too tight. When he and his friends joined them at their table, he teased her, accusing her of everything that was true — that music college would not make her a better singer; that a singer from India should know about Indian music; that her parents would never understand her. As she looks up now from the ants in the dirt, she imagines the contours of happiness. A roof that will never be below water? Too late to ask the drowned people of this valley what exactly was ridiculous about not wanting to leave when the dam was released.

'And what good comes from writing ad slogans?' she had said to him, teasing back, the pub now crowded, her friends and Robert's engrossed in their own conversations.

'No good,' he said, then smiled. He fixed his eyes on her. She swigged the last of her wine without looking away. He was honest; she routinely tumbled towards truth.

Reema looks into the jungle and sees two monkeys perched on a branch. Come, monkey.

Down at the lake, two fishermen's wives wade into the water towards a rock on which clothing is spread. One of the women begins to beat a red garment with a stone. Reema recognises this cloth of her ancestors, knows that the cochineal colour comes from an insect's body. The monkeys scamper at the sound of the rock. Oh, monkey, don't go.

She runs.

In the opposite direction to the monkeys.

Accha is an Indian avowal. She will run, *accha*; she will make a decision, *accha*. The sound is a comma between now and the future.

On the other side of the peninsula, she stops. Her shadow is long and she waves at it, wondering if the others up at the retreat are drinking wine yet or still on tea. If the old man's wife were here, Reema would ask her how it's possible to sleep next to a man, night after night, year after year, and witness as slowly his nostril hair grows longer, his eyebrows run riot across his forehead. She unbuttons her blouse, feeling her chest rise and fall, catching her breath as she slips out of her shorts. She lets her clothes fall onto the veined white stones at her feet. The stones are like flattened pastel marbles, and she can't take her eyes away.

The story of the distant cousin continued throughout Reema's adolescence. Many years on, after the cousin in her arranged marriage had given birth to her sixth girl in a row and all the parents in the Himalayan village pitied the family for the absence of a boy, her husband decided they had to eliminate this new baby. Only then did the cousin allow herself to grieve her true love and his painful death from the kuchala berries. She imagined what her family with him might have been like. She rebelled against her husband's decision to rid them of their shame and enlisted her five other daughters in the cause. The girls threatened their father, refused to eat and did not budge from their baby sister's side, until their father relented. The alarm in Reema's mother's voice, as she told the story, had been for the cousin and her bullying husband, whom she had never loved. But for Reema the real alarm should have been for the sixth girl. What kind of life could she have, knowing that her father had wanted to kill her?

She looks up from the stones towards the lake. A layer of yellow — an oil slick of pollen — lines the shore and makes the water uninviting. No matter. As she walks towards it, she can feel her thighs rub together, plumper there, with plumpness also at her waist. How much of a body is a colony?

She runs into the pine pollen and then dives, *accha*, cold, and bobs up on the other side of it. She shakes her head, wiping the water and pollen from her face. She swims out. The mountains in the distance look closer now, as though perched on the lake itself, the snow line as pronounced as it was when she arrived days ago.

On a tour of the grounds on their first day, the owner told the group that Alexander the Great came to this valley in the third century. Near the sixth-century citadel, he said, Greek pottery and coins are embedded in the lake basin.

But what if there are also bones?

She dips her head beneath the surface and forces her eyes open. In the 1970s when they opened the dam, some oustees had refused to leave and were drowned. She lifts her head out of the water and flips onto her back, raising her arm for the backstroke. Flooding, drowning: this is one way to kill a girl. The Delhi sex selection clinics do not deserve the fees they charge for doing it less dramatically.

Kingfishers flit above her. Hundreds of species of birds have come to replace the thousands of ousted people. Perhaps there is balance.

She is here, after all.

Her father had learned the raga system as a young man in San Francisco and had formed a rock band that used some of the sounds of Carnatic music. He travelled to the south of India to learn more but found himself in Delhi when he needed stable employment, using his Americanness as an advantage. He played only occasionally, without conviction, after he got married and had a family. When he uprooted everyone to London, he stopped listening to music entirely. In college Reema understood the real pull of Carnatic music. And now she will learn the music of Falu and Shankar and Pritam and perhaps she will even sing 'Halka Halka' from his movie and she will be Indian, like her mother, and not confused about anything.

She turns over again and breaststrokes towards the horizon. The sun is lower. She should be heading back. An antelope does not swim. It runs. Robert wants to fly over to meet her in Delhi. But an antelope is always running.

She turns and swims back to the shore, ducking her head under the pollen.

Her clothes are difficult to pull over her wet body. The wedding guests will wonder. She has promised to teach them a canon before dinner. Foolishness. But in truth it's nothing more than a children's round like 'Frère Jacques', which she can make sound like a wedding carillon.

She walks back.

The last fisherman is mooring at the far shore of the inlet. Reema stops on the stones, listens. This might be the moment. She waits for the fisherman to leave his boat and walk up the hill and away.

Nothing is moving. Milk-birds *bloop* from their perches in the forest — their song sounds of milk falling from a cow into a bucket.

She puts her hands on her hips, steadies herself and gets ready.

She screams.

FIVE

Jackson recognises the *bloop*, *bloop* of the milk-bird, the last song of the day from the meadow. A faint cawing from the trees grows distant and human voices rise in its place. He spots two lizards, one after the other, slithering up the cement wall of the lookout. One pauses, suspended diagonally, in wait.

He and the owner of the retreat are standing at the edge of the garden to watch the sunset. But sunsets are as painful as sunrises. There is simply the task at hand. He has been trying to raise the question to Mike of hiring a car and a driver to take him to Varanasi since this afternoon, but now the Ganges doesn't seem the right destination either. He and Amelia never spoke in terms of rebirth or spirit. Mike turns from the orange sun poised above the village on the hill and looks towards the people on the lawn. Jackson follows his gaze.

A few wedding guests are gathered at the yoga shala waiting for the choir rehearsal. Others are seated around the garden in small groups, in hammocks, or by the pool on loungers.

'I know birds better than people,' Mike says, surveying the crowd.

This makes sense. This tall, aloof Brit is a man for animals over people; he'd have to be to live here alone and not be lonely. Jackson nods. 'I know neither.' He laughs; it hurts his ribs, but he

41

mustn't let on, or they will fuss over him again. As they observe the others, Mike delivers his theory of humans through their displays, something it seems he's picked up from his keen attention to wildlife and a mocking awareness of caste and stereotypes. He points out types to Jackson, singling out the wedding guest scrapper, who Mike describes as an ambitious young man who will betray his friends. Then the wedding guest nurse, winning love through giving away too much, and, there, the middle-aged uncle in the plain sherwani who resents his relatives for spending too much money on this party. Jackson laughs heartily, still trying to make up for calling the civet cat ugly. Mike points out Monica, the guest from Canada — determined, but earnest, he says, like the Canadians he met when he travelled across the prairies in the '60s, sleeping in boxcars and hitching rides with long-haul truckers. Inside Jackson a small longing for adventure stirs, but is soon subsumed in the listlessness of another day without her.

Here, on the lookout that hangs over the cliff at the limits of the property, Jackson wonders again if he would ever have been able to build any of this. It takes a dream to belong so fully to a patch of the earth that for forty years you would bring plants from all over the world to it, to a valley that floods and recedes at the mercy of the dam turbine. Amelia, it is something to have a dream.

'What's in those?' he asks Mike, pointing to the beds of vegetables. Mike rattles off names proudly: beetroot, red lettuce, spinach, rocket, red mustard, radish, coriander, parsley, dill, basil, rosemary and two beds of Barot potatoes.

'And over there are my fruit trees: mango, lychee, fig and avocado, the Rangpur tree and the one organic Italian peach.'

Jackson knows a few of the other plants, the flowers that have come from elsewhere: poinsettia, bougainvillea in red, purple, orange, the white of the Madagascan periwinkle, the yellow chrysanthemums, the white crown of thorns blushing pink at their edges.

'Beautiful,' Jackson says.

His neck is also stiff from the fall this morning. He tries to stretch it out, twisting it left, right, left again, and just there he notices Jyoti on her husband's lap in a hammock, her hand at his chest as the two slowly swing.

A fold in her skin at the top of her leg, a honeymoon in Niagara Falls, the back seat of the Studebaker, saliva, beer, the smell of marzipan and semen.

Jackson worries for the young people. He and Mike have lived well, have had adventure, but these young ones are in for interesting times. In the 1970s, when Jackson's company hired drivers to take him to and from dam sites, the roads were full of bicycles and rickshaws, not cars. The half a million who had telephones have become 700 million. India is booming. But across the world the banks have failed and emergency measures have been put in place. Amelia, there is that Chinese curse about interesting times.

'In the autumn, after the monsoon, when the water rises,' Mike says, 'the meadow floods and the basunti flowers float on the top of the reservoir.' He stretches his arm towards the peninsula, indicating the arena of magic.

Jackson looks out into the distance again, but the light is fading. There are flowers that float, Amelia.

More wedding guests gather at the yoga shala, and now Jackson watches Reema organise them. She arranges the shy singers with care, almost tenderness. One young woman wants to stand at the back but Reema coaxes her to the front row. The front row is for the strongest singers, for a body in delight as song moves through it. Amelia should be in the front row.

'Excuse me,' he says to Mike and makes his way to the yoga shala. Sing, Jackson, she would have said.

He taps Reema on the shoulder and she turns. 'I croak worse than the frogs out there,' he says, pointing to the meadow. She smiles and without a word takes his arm to lead him to the back row.

He shares the sheet music with the young woman beside him. On it are simple notes with lyrics he can barely read. They wait for Reema's instructions.

'Warm up the face and the vocal chords will follow,' Reema says, her arms outstretched to welcome them. Her stock first line feels flat to her among all the flowers. Two years of teaching children does not make her an expert. She clears her throat.

Jackson is trapped now, and suddenly feels his mistake. He looks around to find Mike, hoping for rescue, but Mike has turned again to the view. He touches his elbow, which is grazed from his fall. He is intact, but this might be too much: to stand tall, to open his throat in order to make music among these people who have things to live for other than a tea canister. Amelia's voice would have rung out through the valley, in chorus with the birds. He looks at Reema who is still holding her arms up as if in a group hug, waiting for them all to settle in. She opens her mouth wide then long, baring her teeth, inviting them to do the same. She scrunches up her nose towards her eyes, makes pulsing trumpets with her lips. They follow.

Reema watches Jyoti's cousins giggle at the faces they're pulling. She looks from one singer to the next, to encourage them to copy her. These are not people used to being silly in front of others; they guard their faces like their jewels. Only Monica is different. Reema has some distance to really take her in. Her wavy hair, brown skin, round belly. Monica follows instructions dutifully. She exaggerates the movement of her mouth, reveals herself, unashamed.

'Ooo oooo ooo,' Reema sings, then quickly follows with a hiccupping 'ah, ah,' up and down the scale. And again.

Jackson pretends to make the sounds, but the other wedding guests now begin to take it seriously and their ah ah ahs get louder.

'Vvvv,' Reema shouts, 'Vvv … vvvv … vvv …' and they all follow. 'Jj,' she says next, 'Jj … jj … jj … jj …' and the cousins and new in-laws are getting the hang of this. Together they are a meadow creature. Reema holds on to the tail of sound and lets herself go, in her element now.

'Drop your shoulders — it helps,' she says, and this Jackson does. But suddenly the dread reappears and the sight of her face and shoulders shames him. He slouches and looks for a vacant chair, but they are all taken up by Jyoti's family who have gathered around the shala, eager to hear the English music. Women fan themselves; a small child circles her father like an airplane, arms raised above her head.

Leaves spin like helicopter blades from the branches of trees. Gold, red, crusty, withered brown. We call it fall here, not autumn, the teacher says, correcting me, but the Alberta boys have not finished laughing. English boy's blazer, shorts, the brown knee socks with purple stripes, and oh Mother how could you have sent me out like this, the wind disrobing

trees, my bottom thudding when they push me hard so that I land in a
crisp brown pile on the pavement they call a sidewalk.

———

At the end of the rehearsal Reema keeps her eyes on the bamboo
floor of the shala, breathing her way back from the music. She looks
up towards the reservoir just as the sunset ties a sash around the lake.
The rehearsal has gone better than she imagined it would, and she
has to admit that she loved the sounds as they came together. Jyoti
had suggested a madrigal for lovers, but with a group of amateurs,
few who could read music or reach notes or keep rhythms, Reema
chose an easy traditional canon. *Dona nobis pacem.* Grant us peace,
yes. And now that they've made it through rehearsal — three words
sung over and over again in a round — she feels less irritable.

The first choir she ever led was at college; Saturday afternoons
with fellow students. She challenged them to believe they could learn
difficult music and eventually perform in public. Her mates slowly
stopped coming and, in the end, the last three singers eventually
decided that Saturdays were for shops and bars. Reema's leadership,
they said, lacked conviction. For girls like them, along with most of
the women at this wedding, singing is an unnecessary distraction
from what they might consume. Perhaps it's those who have little
or nothing who need to sing and sing and sing, and perhaps she
is devoted to the sounds themselves. She's satisfied that with the
wedding guests she was in control, and *Do-ona no-obis pa-cem pa-
cem* made it easy for them to sound like a real choir. Jyoti will be
pleased, and after the performance Reema can make her excuses to

head north at her own pace, airing out her thoughts before she visits her mother's family. She gathers the sheet music and smiles as the singers leave the shala. Jackson remains in his spot.

'How are you feeling?' she asks him, moving closer.

Nutmeg. He opens his eyes at the tease of a smell that makes him consider following it. Ah, that's a thing to remember: to hold his breath more often to stop life flowing in. He looks into her face, wondering what he's missed. Has he slept? He has an inkling that things have gone on around him.

He straightens his shirt. Her eyes are kind. He touches her hand, which rests on his forearm.

'Just checking. Was it too much?' she says.

Not too much, not the effort to make a sound, but it's too much, yes, every day, merely to wake up.

'I think the civet cat got my tongue!' he says. She smiles. 'Awfully hot,' he adds, and yes, Amelia, you caught him at it again, making a joke when he should answer the question.

'Have you seen the fish that eats birds?' Reema says.

The young woman's marbled eyes flash at him with such force that he has to blink, and this, he remembers, is the way every man in every land, in every era, feels his appetite even after it has passed.

'Mike says that in that pond over there is a big yellow fish. He's seen it leap out of the water and catch a bird,' she says, pointing across the garden.

'Oh?' Appetite is strange across species, Amelia.

'It happens early in the morning — I'm going watch for it tomorrow,' Reema says.

Jackson stares at the pond, waiting for the fish to jump. Is it possible to die of longing? Surely it's the only thing we die of. Amelia's asthma made her prone to the bronchitis that caused the pneumonia that triggered the septicaemia that took her away in tiny strokes that closed her brain.

'My wife,' he starts, but can't remember what he was going to say. Can he trust her?

Twelve years old, hot legs, sticky vinyl car seat, Dad beside the Venezuelan driver, up the hill, Sinclair Oil Refinery over the peak, but the driver stops on the incline, steals Dad's wallet and leaves us at the side of the road as the car slides backwards down the hill.

Reema pats his arm.

'My wife would have loved your choir,' he says, coming back.

'Thank you.' She pauses, would like to say more, but old men are a mystery. She squeezes his arm slightly before she walks towards the veranda.

Jackson watches Mike and the long-haired man cross her path as they come towards him. The young man steps lightly. His arms and legs are long and lithe, his face wide and fresh.

'Feeling better?' the young man asks as they arrive beside Jackson. He lands on the last step as though dropped there on a breeze.

'This is Yosh,' Mike says, 'He leads our yoga retreats and has come to work for Jyoti's guests.'

The three of them stand silently at first, then slowly find the threads of a conversation, as though it rises from the flowers. Yosh is young but he speaks like he is used to being among men of a greater age, with deep knowledge of the area. Mike alludes to places they have in common, to Dharamkot where it turns out the yogi did his training.

Yosh tells them that in Talwara yesterday there was an accident in which a truck hit a man who had come to kayak at the reservoir. The kayaker is in hospital and the village must pray that he lives.

'He is American. There will be bad press,' Yosh says.

Jackson watches Yosh grip his left wrist with his right hand, standing straighter. He is a different kind of Indian altogether. Even with all the years Jackson has spent in India there are still codes among men here that he will never decipher.

When he and Amelia visited Deepak and his family for a millennium New Year's Eve celebration in Delhi, they met a man, Ashok Parmar — he will never forget that name — who was the president of a company that made platforms for oil rigs in the sea. The other guests at the party eyed him with suspicion and even disdain, but Amelia was drawn to him, chatted to him as the clock moved towards midnight. The man carried two pens in his jacket pocket. Just after midnight, he ceremoniously pulled out both pens in order to demonstrate to the revellers that now that their computer systems had survived into the year 2000 the new era would be different. Amelia watched him, intrigued. The green pen, Parmar told them, was the one he bought in 1973 when he had to appear for his class eleven board exam and didn't have the four annas it cost to replace the nib. His teacher had to give him the money so that he could take the exam. The other one was a Mont Blanc pen worth 80,000 rupees, with which he now signed cheques for his 200 employees. The man had been from a scheduled caste and had risen to wealth thanks to economic reform. The circle of engineers and their wives were reluctantly impressed, and Amelia's face betrayed that she'd been charmed.

This yogi's face is like Ashok Parmar's, challenging, yet unguarded. Jackson sees that he is distracted by the young women on the terrace, even as his body appears straight and present, rubbing his wrist.

'Any news on the court cases?' Mike says.

'They have a new lawyer,' Yosh says. 'They need more representation — that's the only way to fight at this point.'

'They?' Jackson asks.

'The oustees,' Yosh says.

So this, Jackson realises, is the news of the season: the oustees from the Pong Dam project have renewed their legal battle for compensation. And this young man seems to know the lawyers and the leaders. This has happened with many a dam, time and again, as he has learned from articles he read when he visited the library with Amelia back home and sat down to read the *Hindustan Times*. The insurgents are disruptive Maoists.

Talwara was founded on the dam — built to house its engineers and construction workers. Jackson has lived in many a town such as this, has seen the hand of progress, and it's not one that slackens its grip.

He becomes hot, turns to find some breeze.

'The choirmaster's family are local,' Mike adds, and all three men look towards the veranda where Reema is talking to Jyoti's mother, crouched beside her, smiling, encouraging the mother's pride in her daughter.

'She is barely Indian,' Yosh says, and Jackson wonders if this is accusation or compliment. The young man now massages the muscle at the top of his arm. He seems anxious and Jackson notes that his eyes are still on the pair of women on the veranda. It's no surprise that this handsome man would feel the pull of such a beautiful woman.

'And you? Where are you from?' he asks Yosh.

'Originally from a village in Maharashtra.'

Jackson is sure that Ashok Parmar was from the same state. Parmar's pens marked his ascent in the world; he wanted his children to have an education. He sent his son to a private Jesuit institution in Mumbai, to study with boys from higher castes. He'd told Amelia, as the new millennium dawned, that he wanted his children to learn what it meant to be a Dalit, to come from one life only to lead a new and better one.

'Are you a family of yogis?' Jackson asks, his eyes on the man's strong shoulder. Amelia, young people are so beautiful.

'No yogis, no.'

'I can't touch my knees,' Jackson says. He leans forward to indulge in the joke but feels his bladder urging as he bends. He straightens quickly. 'What does your father do?'

Yosh hesitates. 'Why do you ask?'

'I used to work in that state,' Jackson says.

Yosh finally turns his gaze from the veranda. 'Shoes. He has a factory.'

Jackson nods. He knows which castes work with leather, and those that refuse to.

Yosh turns back towards the veranda.

'She was the only one on the meadow this afternoon,' Mike says. His eyes have also been on Reema. 'It must have been her who screamed bloody murder.'

Jackson glances again at Reema. He feels cold now. He notices that the laces on his canvas shoes have come loose. He checks his fly. He's always catching it open, but no, this time it's zipped.

The rows of pinnis, balushahis and gur ka halwa, the cauldrons of samosas, the rickshaw, the Golden Temple and the men with tents in their kurtas, the woman, their laughter, I freeze.

'Her father was a famous musician in California in the '70s,' Mike says. 'Her brother is a lawyer in London.' He bends down to pick up a blossom that has blown from a tree and Jackson watches him roll it in his fingers like a cigar. Mike is a refined man who knows cigars and flowers, as well as civet cats.

Jackson focuses on the grass in front of him, the small insects that flit and stumble over one another. In the distance he hears a pop. 'Ah, champagne,' he says, as he looks up.

Panama. The basin of the Rio Chagres, phosphorescent blue light end of day as we make our way up to the engineer's tent, her belly and hips before me on the trail swollen with what I put there, and I am proud and jealous at the same time, and is that why it didn't stay?

'Who got the oustees the new lawyers?' Mike asks, and his voice brings Jackson back to the garden.

'Sharma led the whole petition himself,' Yosh says.

'But there are a hundred thousand claimants,' Mike says.

Jackson touches his belt, checks his fly again. He needs to time the urgings of his bladder correctly to make it across the garden without an accident.

'With no electricity or water,' Yosh says.

Jackson watches as Mike uses his other hand to roll the flower in his palm.

While Jackson worked on the Rio Chagres, in Panama, the Indian government was making plans for the Narmada River. Thirty big dams, hundreds of medium dams, thousands of smaller ones. He remembers feeling jealous of the possibilities the Narmada brought, the largest dam eventually rising to five hundred and thirty feet. But the disputes — for ownership, for territory, for rights, for water, for the power generated by the water — these he's happy to have avoided. His engineering colleagues wrote to him of the controversy. Morarji Desai had told the valley people, *If you move it will be good. Otherwise we shall release the waters and drown you all.*

'Sometimes these things can't be helped,' Jackson says, but he sees that this has come out wrong.

'So you say,' Yosh says as he leans slightly back.

Mike throws the blossom on the grass and rubs his hands through his hair. He rolls up the sleeves of his shirt. 'I'd better see what's happening with dinner,' he announces and walks away. Jackson has missed his chance to go alongside him.

'India has made great progress,' Jackson says.

Yosh leaves enough silence for Jackson to hear the ring of cliché in his words and the divide between him and this man. 'I suppose it depends on what you mean by progress,' Jackson adds. More silence. 'There is excellent business in shoes.'

Yosh looks at him. 'My father was poor,' Yosh says.

'Yes, of course.'

'We moved to Delhi when I was twelve,' Yosh continues, making the point that Jackson cannot get away with only pleasantries. 'I went to school there. I went to college in New York. I've lived in London, New York, the Midwest, and now Vancouver. People in those places are no different …'

'What do you mean?' Jackson says as music starts from the veranda, the bass beat announcing that it will be another night of dancing.

'I mean, here we all are.'

The volume is turned up on the music.

Jackson has lived in more places, but out of them all, he counts India as formative and yet elusive. He got his first job as an engineer because his father knew the chief executive of the Bhakra Dam. In 1948, in the wake of Partition in the Punjab, Jackson stayed, found another job, because he could be counted on to be a quiet, dutiful intern with a penchant for adventure and yet respect for local custom. To be in the same country in the same month as the last breaths of Gandhi — now that was —

The alley, the protruding kurta, the men huddled.

'Dalit people like my family can be rich now,' Yosh says. 'My father built a shoe company thanks to economic reforms. Is that progress? He lives in Delhi. People love him for his money, but he can't sleep without getting drunk every night.'

Jackson watches Yosh shift from side to side, glancing over at the dancing on the veranda but stuck here with this old fool.

'The Bhakra Dam is concrete,' Jackson says, 'but the dam here is earth-filled. There's a big difference …' But this makes no sense, even to him, never mind impressing the young man. Jackson's father made him go to India for his first internship, when Jackson wanted to go nowhere at all, wanted to stay still and not uproot his life every time there was oil in a new country. He wanted to stop ending things with girls he'd barely kissed. You love your parents, you hate your parents, then you become them and know that you must forgive them.

'Excuse me, Mr Baines,' Yosh says. 'I think they want us to go up for champagne,' and he moves off in the direction of the young people on the veranda.

Jackson is weary. In the months after Amelia passed away, the doctor told him with a straight face, no hint of irony, that the ECG tests indicated that his heart had lost some capacity. If there is anything he can teach a young person it is not to take things too seriously. Laugh. Play. And don't hold on so tight, he would have told any child of his. And don't be bullheaded or arrogant or think you know anything at all.

Amelia, he has no one to forgive him.

Six

She doesn't like the fizz of champagne, but Reema holds out her glass.

'Just a bit,' she says, seated in the rattan armchair in the corner of the veranda. 'I have to work, thanks to you,' she adds, as she allows Jyoti to pour from the bottle of Moët.

Women's voices from the other side of the veranda are grating. They are practising the canon. *Do-na, no-bis* ... They stop, giggle. There are women who do not like to take themselves seriously, she knows, as she watches the bubbles build in the glass. She is too intense for most of the women here. Many have remarked on the colour of her skin, clearly unaware of her half-white father. They want to know which products she has used: Palmer's or Clear Essence? In India she is white enough to be a Bollywood star. In London she is black enough to be suspect. *Accha.*

She holds up her hand to stop Jyoti from filling her glass. During the wedding only tiny sips of champagne passed her lips. Each time the glass was refilled she tipped it out into the fish pond. Don't leap, fishy.

'She's complaining about there not being enough food,' Jyoti says, still pouring. Reema watches, thinking that if she tips her glass over the banister and laughs at the same time, she can lose nearly half of it.

Jyoti discusses her new mother in-law as though the woman

in the bright blue sari and the finest jewelled stilettos in Himachal Pradesh is not within hearing distance. Although both of them have been as gracious with each other as they can be, Jyoti is on edge, rolling her eyes in her presence and trying to gather sympathy from her side of the wedding party.

'*Is* there enough food?' Reema says.

Jyoti stares at her with shock and stops pouring.

'Wasn't it at least one village-sized portion per person?' Reema says. She keeps a straight face, daring herself to continue, to confess her thoughts: that Jyoti's in-laws are rich and modern and at least she is not in service to them, what with her dowry in the form of a degree in medicine. At least this bride feels at home in the new India. She relents. 'Don't be so touchy — I'm teasing,' she says.

Jyoti tilts the bottle and fills the glass right to rim, as though to challenge her, but there's no way she could know.

'I'm sorry,' Reema says.

Jyoti holds the champagne bottle in both hands like a trophy. 'Are you okay?'

'Completely okay,' Reema says and takes a big gulp.

'Have you spoken to Robert? He should be here,' Jyoti says, accusingly, then smiles and moves on to pour for the others on the veranda. Jyoti disapproves of Robert, finds him unsophisticated, but likes that he makes a good income and can spot them rounds at the Crown.

Reema tunes into footfalls on the pebbles around the veranda, positioned to make noise to ward off snakes. Bhangra music floats in from the village on the other side of the reservoir when there's a break in the techno soundtrack from the veranda, where Jyoti's

London friends have been queuing up music for the evening. Reema stares after Jyoti — a model of how to make the world do as you wish it to.

'And for you?' Jyoti asks Jackson. He raises his hand, declining. 'I saw you rehearsing,' she says, with the softness Reema knows she needs to learn. 'Thank you, thank you so much for everything you've done to be here,' she says, and she leans in and kisses Jackson's cheek. It is easy to be generous when you follow the path and the path even bends for you. When your mind doesn't circle on the drowned bodies on the riverbank. Still, Reema needn't have been so brittle with the old man. She is not herself. All this *accha*.

In the dusk, the trees around the veranda are like cut-out silhouettes. Jyoti's family are huddled around a laptop, watching video footage of the wedding. The friends drink quickly and plenty. *Besharam*, Reema wants to say, but she must stop pretending that she can think in Hindi or reason convincingly in English. See no … Speak no … Hear no … The smells coming from the kitchen give her a rush of nausea, so she stands up to catch some of the breeze above the railing.

'Join you?' she asks Jackson, once she gets her balance.

'Of course,' he says and starts to shunt down on the rattan sofa.

'Don't move, plenty of room,' she says, and squeezes herself in at the end, her leg touching his knee. Someone laughs like the Queen of the Night and Reema searches among the cousins for the face belonging to that voice.

'Well, this is grand, isn't it?' Jackson says, as he feels her smooth arm on his.

'I'm starving,' she says, trapped in the tiny space between his bony knee and the edge of the sofa. He shifts farther away and turns towards her.

'The choir sounded beautiful by the end. They will make you proud tonight, with no thanks to me,' he says. He raises his hand to scratch the grizzle around his neck, coaxing a smile. 'They say if you need a mountain moved, get the smallest, most angry person to push first.'

She feels the sting, sits straighter and draws her knee away from his. She looks towards Jyoti's older cousins, wondering if she should invent a skincare product to discuss with them.

A small child cries out over the lawn.

'I'm used to teaching children, mostly,' she says, attempting not to resent him. She didn't force him to sing.

Her friends at college are good teachers not because they are good singers, but because they want nothing more than to be teachers. They are patient; they care about passing along their knowledge and talent. Perhaps they even have grandparents they have learned how to be patient from, whereas Reema has none. Her English grandfather was known for performing his bullying silently from a small dark room at the back of the house in Fremont, California, while his Goan wife cooked and Reema's father studied mathematics instead of the music he loved. Is there a gene for patience that she is missing? Sadhana says that prajna should be her only goal as a singer — wisdom that is higher than knowledge. Yes, that.

She and Jackson share another thick, uneasy moment. She wonders what he is seeing. Once at Trinity College of Music a teacher told her that her head was the wrong shape for a singer. What is it the right shape for? She has been told she should model, or act. No one has said you should become a professional singer and hold the world in the palm of your hand. No one has ever said that when you hold it, you will change it, you will ease suffering. She looks around again for the source of the crazy laugh.

'Was it you?' he asks as he lets his knee fall towards hers, just short of contact.

'What do you mean?' Old men have been known to read minds. Her mother once told her a story of their great-great-uncle who predicted a robbery at his musical instrument shop because he had read in his customer's mind that he was measuring the doorway in relation to the instruments themselves. The next day three sitars, ten bansuri and as many dhadd were missing, the door frame shattered, because the customer's inner measuring tape was inaccurate.

'It sounded like a woman — that scream from the meadow,' he says.

'It did, yes. Strange.' She looks into his eyes, which are cloudy but knowing. Both of her grandfathers died before she was born, and while her mother's father's passing — swift, after a fall from a ladder — has been elevated to the level of myth similar to that of Reema's birth, the only time her father spoke well of his own father was as she held his hand in hospital before his angioplasty two years ago. There are things to learn from a generation she has little experience of. What will Robert be like as an old man? Robert, who doesn't read books or listen to opera and yet is the happiest man she has ever known. Someone will have to pity him when he is old and weak. Pity is what keeps old people alive, and perhaps it doesn't run in her family. 'Sometimes the monkeys can sound very human,' she says.

He smiles at her like a great uncle who reads minds. She laughs. 'I saw a snake. Can't stand them,' she says, just short of a confession.

His eyes twinkle. 'I understand.' He sits back against the sofa, as though this seeing inside someone has exhausted him.

'How are you feeling?'

'Yes, well ... In Italian they say *a poco a poco ... Al fine!*' and he laughs.

With Jackson's head on her lap, his body splayed out, his trousers soaked in urine, Reema had felt time disappear. 'And did you get a chance to rest? The heat is intense in the afternoon,' she says.

'I have been thinking about what you said,' the old man says.

She must think of him with his name. Jackson. Jackson is surely different from her grandfather who drank until he died of a haemorrhage in the dark room in Fremont. 'I think you're angry with me for something I said about the dam,' he says.

'No, no,' she says, bobbing her head side to side like her grandmother does and *accha* she is Indian after all. 'I'm not angry.'

'I have no children — I don't know how to talk to young people.'

'There is no trick,' she says. 'You just have to remember that they only think about themselves.' She's surprised by how true this sounds.

'My wife,' he says, but hesitates. 'She's with me.' They look at each other in a silence that coincides with a lull in the veranda music and chatter. He waits until there is more background noise before he continues. 'Not the way you think,' he says, touching the spot on his chest near his heart, 'but that's also true.' He looks around to make sure no one else can hear. 'She is in my suitcase.'

Reema holds her breath.

'Will you help me?' he says.

Seven

Kneeling in front of the wall on her side of the room, Reema places her hands on the rug the way she's seen the others do on the yoga mats, palms flat, shoulder-distance apart. She lowers the top of her head to the floor and puts her weight on it, lifting her bottom in the air, straightening her legs. She did this as a child.

She kicks up one foot then the other, and both crash back down. She tries again. And again. A brief moment of inversion is all she wants. Things will revert to normal. Upside down is right side up now. Backwards is forwards. She kicks up both legs and her feet hit the wall; the top of her head feels like it will crack open and her neck strains.

The door opens.

'How's it going?' Monica says.

Reema drops her feet to the floor and sits up.

'Yeah, great,' she says.

Monica doesn't miss a beat — nothing to see here — as she puts her bag on the bed and kicks off her shoes. She turns to her suitcase on the floor, taking out a few items. She unfolds them, folds them back up carefully again.

Reema gets up and busies herself, tidying. Monica's side of the room is ordered, while Reema has spilled the contents of her backpack out onto the floor and the bed, and scattered her toiletries and underwear around the bathroom. Sprawling, expanding, layers and layers of herself. Monica is Canadian, the kind of Indian cousin unused to chaos, the one for whom Delhi is a shock.

'I like toilet paper in my washrooms,' Monica told her the first night they were together in this room, going into detail about some of the pit stops she'd made to get here and the toilets she'd been in, struggling with faucets, hoses, and the absence of paper. As Reema listened, marking Monica's wide Canadian vowels, she imagined the woman's arrival in Delhi, the taxi from the airport, the constant honking of horns, the diffuse Delhi light. Monica, an amateur photographer, had guided Reema's attention to the difference in the light in India, along with the vehicles, the disordered weaving of scooters, autorickshaws, and rickshaws through the streets lined with rubbish and sleeping cows.

'I live near the lake,' Monica said, and she described how she walked to work and to her workouts at the gym along Toronto streets that followed straight lines. Monica is a marker of lines of light, angles, and gaps in order, her ancestors' caste long-dissolved in her education and dreams to succeed. Reema understood how this kind of cousin could be at once enchanted and yet disgusted by the sight of Delhi. Reema was born in India, but when Monica told her about the shops she'd been to in Delhi, the forts, the tombs and the gardens, Reema felt outdone.

'I bought something in Delhi that I'm going to wear for the performance,' Monica says, unfolding a bag from her suitcase.

Still, if Reema had known that Monica was taking the same train to Pathankot, she would have been happy for the company. She herself had arrived at the station in Delhi early, suddenly aware of her clothes, her hair, the way she moved, and that it was mostly only the men in the station who took note of her. She covered her head with her shawl and stood near the toilets where a few children slept. A man relieved himself just outside the doors, not bothering with a urinal, while families sat on the floor near the trickling urine and unwrapped steaming food from delicate foil parcels.

She'd decided she should wait in the café on the first floor. She pushed past people coming towards her on the platform, a crush of women with cloth-wrapped bundles on their backs, boxes on their heads, heavy suitcases, men sharing the weight of a trunk, stray children threading their way among the hundreds of legs. As she walked towards the stairs, she felt a tug at the base of her backpack, like a mouse gnawing at the nylon. The feeling was distinctly eerie. When she reached the café and took off her backpack, she saw the slit in the front compartment. She had worn a money belt for her passport and cash, and her phone had been buried deep within her clothes, but the slit from the knife had released her iPod into the hands of a thief, and now she had none of her music. Being a target for a Delhi thief had shamed her. She was a rich foreigner now, not a local, and could not be at home in the city of her birth.

She watches Monica carefully lift more items from her suitcase. Would Monica have had her pack slit at the train station? She's a New World Indian who walks around with a camera strung around her neck like the most obvious of American tourists.

Reema shoves the dirty clothes from her railway journey into the bottom of her pack. She will need to do laundry. The nine hours overnight from Delhi to Pathankot were sleepless. The air conditioning in the first-class cars of the Dhauladhar Express seemed to have long-ago broken down, and there were stains along the seats and compartment walls that only heat, dirt and body oils could have produced. The stains gave her an odd, familiar comfort; she was in the right place, in this women-only compartment. But across from her on the upper berth was a middle-aged man, with his wife and teenage daughter cuddled together on the berth below him.

'What are you doing here?' she barked at the man in Hindi. When he shrugged and wrapped the brown woollen Indian Railways issue blanket around his bare feet, the daughter let loose a tirade of who-do-you-think-you-are, among other insults Reema didn't have enough language to understand, let alone retaliate with. The woman on the bunk below Reema's was a Swedish backpacker who said nothing to any of them. Where was Monica on that train? Would she have spoken up and asked the man to leave?

The man snored throughout the night, keeping Reema awake. In the blackness and the sawing of breath that smelled like rotten eggs, she crept from her bunk, put a shawl over her head, and, carrying her backpack with her, went into the corridor. Near one of the doors between compartments she set her pack on the floor, sat down and leaned against it, resting her head. Lights went on and off, doors opened, men walked past her in the darkness. Some tried to talk to her; others cursed her; a few seemed to pity her. Of course, she had made a mistake being in the corridor in the middle of the night. Then the yellowed clipping about the murdered Keralan woman on a train, sent by her father, came to her mind. Reema took herself back to the compartment and endured the snorts and grunts more easily, like one of the family. When she was picked up at the Pathankot station the next morning by Jyoti's college friend, who had volunteered to meet her and Monica, her clothes smelled of urine.

On the floor beside her bed now, she spots a small piece of lined paper with neat handwriting. At the top centre of the paper there is a black and orange illustration of a clock. She picks it up. Names of tourist attractions in Northern India and their approximate distance from Delhi; a list of phone numbers next to names and descriptions of relations ('Dad's second cousin'; 'Mom met their father in Montreal'); a list of yoga styles and associated teachers. Reema cannot fathom why people need to do so much, see so much, buy so much.

'Is this yours?' she asks and holds it up.

Monica turns. 'Oh there it is,' she says, taking it from Reema, sheepishly. 'I'm lost without lists.' She folds up the paper, opens the top drawer of the rosewood dresser, lifts out a magenta pashmina still in its clear plastic wrapping and places the list beneath it. She takes her choice of clothing into the bathroom.

When Monica emerges a few minutes later, she is wearing shalwar, not with a kameez but with a tank top. Reema tries not to look too carefully at the awkward combination, because, after all, who is she to say what's the right way to wear Indian clothes.

'A different look for me,' Monica says. Reema knows that Monica is a banker. She pictures the financial sector uniforms — the tights and smart heels, a delicate string of pearls to set the look off — that Monica is probably used to. Wearing shalwar would feel daring.

'You look great,' Reema says.

Monica looks down at the folded layers of fabric falling to her ankles and then back at Reema. She shrugs.

'I was fired from my job,' she says.

There's a long pause between them as the news lingers in the air for interpretation. Reema waits.

'My company had a ninety per cent profit drop during the fourth quarter last year.' More of a pause as the insects sing. 'They gave me a box for my things.' Monica throws up her hands in an *oh well*, then pulls the tank top down, over the waist of the shalwar, and ties the strings tighter. She leaves the room.

Reema sits on the bed. An office job would make her want to set fire to something. If she had to work in an office, she is sure she would smoke, ruin her voice, her skin, her teeth. Her brother is a lawyer who works with bankers. In the last few months he has phoned her with stories of events in the States. 'One inelegant rogue French trader,' he said, 'and the banking industry is in crisis.' She is only beginning to understand the economics of it, through names like Lehman Brothers twinned with the alarm in her brother's voice. He told her about his close friend who received her notice to leave in the first days of the crisis but wouldn't come out of her office. Reema imagined this woman her own age lying down on a grey carpet that smelled like vomit, curling up over her handbag, kicking off her court heels and letting the hole in her tights spread down her thigh as she lifted her knees to her chest. Reema has seen television clips of men in suits walking out of an office with their heads hung, carrying boxes of their belongings. But that image — of a woman in the foetal position on a carpet, with a wide tear in her stocking lengthening imperceptibly with each sob — makes her sad, and yet secretly triumphant over everything she and her brother ever argued about.

She looks out of the window of her room. Lemon trees, amaryllis blossoms. She thinks about the bulbul that perches on the railing of the veranda at breakfast waiting for scraps.

———

Anchor butter — that was the best, from New Zealand; we even had Anchor butter in Venezuela before the war, but after the war the Brits stopped subsidising New Zealand and the company nearly went bust. I was a man when the war ended, saved pennies to eat meals off campus, never found Anchor butter, and my best friend had to go back to live with his folks. After the war everyone was bust.

EIGHT

Reema stands in the night air on the lookout where insects fling themselves at the tiny fairy lights lining the railing. Creatures move, people move, something is always born, something always dies. She strains her eyes to see if she can locate the rotting carcass on the meadow. She thinks she spots it, but then the thing darts across the grass swiftly and her heart leaps. If change is slow, like the crawl of evolution, there's time to adapt. But sometimes change sneaks up, is brutal, is obliterating. Her body is a valley; her body is a river; her body will change. There, she's certain she sees it: the inert calf, forsaken on the grass.

Mike told her that before the Beas River was flooded and this reservoir created, only catfish, mirror carp and other coarse fish meandered between the pink and white stones on the riverbed. Now the reservoir is full of silver carp, rohu, and mahseer. Some fishermen have a vibrant trade. And birds have come.

She has challenged herself to learn some names of creatures and plants in Hindi, but she cannot remember them, can only remember what Mike told her in English. Lapwings, pintails, cormorants, grebes, plovers, terns, egrets, in greater numbers every year. A flood took place. Birds came. The photographs her father sent her of the drowned houses and the cracked earth in drought — *these*, he must have been saying, these are the ways of the world, the violent ways that you must protect yourself from. And *these*, thank you Father, she said to herself as she placed the photographs on her bedside table, are what you should have been sending my brother too, all these years. Her brother is selfish and richer by the day. He doesn't disturb his wealth by holding story upon story in his heart. When her mother speaks of lost cousins, Reema knows that they all surely cannot be cousins, but just as surely, something always dies, something is always born.

She hears men's voices from the centre of the garden, turns and sees Mike and the yoga teacher in the dark by the fountain, outside the spill of the solar lights that line the gravel path. She listens. They discuss the classes for the next two days, the planned excursions — the end of this long wedding week in sight.

'Can I book you in for September, group of fifteen?' Mike asks the yoga teacher.

'Of course. Hatha?'

'Whatever you like. They're a group from New York. Their teacher broke her leg,' Mike says.

Reema steps closer to hear better, but stays hidden behind the mango tree.

'Are you sure you want me?' Yosh says. 'American teachers may bring their students to India but the students can't imagine doing yoga with an Indian.'

The few yoga classes that Reema has been to in London have been the hardest exercise she has ever done. Yoga to a bass beat — a soundtrack not unlike an aerobics class, but quieter. The instructors did countdowns and called out encouragement — *find peace where there is no peace*. She was a peace soldier in boot camp. In one class, after months of enduring the teacher, who told them he'd been a dancer, and who wore beautiful leggings and a headband, she pulled a muscle while holding the plough position. The teacher instructed the class to move their legs up and down, and to count backwards from *twenty, nineteen, eighteen*. And again. Pulsing to *find that peace where there is no peace, you can do it, come on ladies and gentlemen*. With three oms to finish. Namaste. A greeting that felt like an insult after all the pulsing torture. She soon quit.

'The groups love you. You're different,' Mike says.

Reema catches sight of a mongoose that slips below the fence and out into the night meadow.

'Do they?' Yosh says.

'You're the real thing,' Mike says.

'In the west they don't care about Dalits adjusting them in downward dog.' Reema hears the bitterness in Yosh's tone. 'But I don't think they want the real thing,' he says.

'Will you do it?'

'I need the money,' Yosh says, 'I turn thirty in a few months.'

'And?'

'Time to stop relying on my father.'

'I thought you did that long ago,' Mike says.

'Not entirely.'

Yosh seems bold and shy at once, timid but also confident. He reminds Reema of the tabla player from that night at the Southbank Centre, whose playing appeared so deceptively technical until she realised it had taken over her body.

In music college, she was often bored, wanting more out of the course, more of a challenge to her voice. She knew she was never going to be a star, but she wanted to dream. She would often wander into music events, randomly. One time, she saw Patri Satish Kumar, a musician her father had once mentioned. Despite everything he despised India for, he said, the subcontinent still produced the best musicians. This young Kumar was a maverick on the mridangam, her father said, but he still showed high respect for the centuries of mridangam players that came before him.

The low-level stage was set with three microphones no higher than two feet off the floor, ready for performers who would sit cross-legged on traditional woven rugs. When Kumar arrived on stage, she felt surprised by his handsomeness. He sat behind the mridangam, and was joined by an older man on the tavil and a young man who took up the khanjira. Their first piece was as she'd expected, tabla rhythms that felt as though they were split or frayed, like cloth that had once been whole. The playing was steady and yet furious in moments. She followed the subtle up and down of a narrative line, but she couldn't trace the story, couldn't find the five movements, or any way of being sustained. She searched for the one beat and tried to keep time in measures she knew weren't 4/4 or even 9/8 but still she searched: One, no, not there, One, two, no. One. She endured the sounds, certain that she would never find the appeal of this music. The man on the khanjira began to sing: *Takadadada takadadada da da tak tak takada* … and on and on, and still she could not find the arc. She decided she would leave after the piece ended and calculated the number of people along the row she would have to disturb to pass. She refocused on *the Takada takada takada, da da, takada tak* and a feeling began to emerge. She swayed; the percussion built, and she marvelled at the speed at which Kumar's hands moved on the mridangam. Not only his hands, but his fingers, making nearly imperceptible beats without air or time between them, forming a pulse. She was inside the beat without counting, and up and down the dynamics she travelled. At the dramatic end, several in the crowd *whooed* at the last slap of the tablas. She wanted to *whoo*, too, but restrained herself. The audience applauded and she joined them, deciding she would stay for the next piece. The next and the next. Nearly an hour later, still mesmerised by the hands and fingers, the pulsing they set off in her chest, she felt the concert come to an end with a *pap pap pap*. Up into the air flew the drummers' hands on the final beat. She rose to her feet and *whooed* with the rest.

It was later that night, at home alone in her Kilburn flat, that she felt so lonely she searched online for an Indian music teacher.

She hears Yosh give Mike directions to a carpenter in the area who will help with some repairs, and looks up to see that the choir has begun to assemble at the shala. She slips around the mango tree and heads towards the perimeter of the garden, giving Mike and Yosh a wide berth. When she reaches the gravel path, the sound of her steps gives her away, but she doesn't look back. She climbs the steps to the shala, then goes to stand at the podium, where she smiles at the singers who gather in the places she assigned them this afternoon.

She drops her chin to her chest, releasing tension in her neck, and takes a deep breath. She's expecting the back row to come in first, so she looks up and catches their eyes. '*Do-na* ... *No-bis* ... *Pacem* ... *Pa-cem*,' she mouths to them. She listens for a lull in the noises from the night meadow and doesn't think about anything drowned or rigid. She concentrates on the music in front of her, on the time signature, and then on images of running fawns, nymphs of peace. When she hears the struggling voices of the choir she will try not to hear the clash of this kind of music with this environment. She will try not to feel ridiculous.

Monica arrives, apologising for being late. Reema smiles and wonders what other secrets Monica holds and whether she might be someone to talk to. She appears to stay on the surface of things, but there is much more going on there. When she takes her place in the second row, all twelve singers are assembled.

Solar fairy lights twinkle along the railing of the shala and the moon is on its back over the reservoir.

'Eeeeayyahhhoouuuu,' Reema sings as warm-up. The singers echo her; they understand the importance of vowels from rehearsal. She repeats it. A few of the men and Monica to the right of them are ragged and sharp. She examines their stance. Monica now has her thin singlet tucked into the waist of the shalwar, with the strings hanging down in front of her crotch and thighs. The Indian nanis might have a thing or two to say about this, accusing Monica of asking for someone to pull that string. But Reema likes that Monica's clothes do not match, do not fit quite right, and that Monica does not seem to notice.

Reema looks at Jackson in the back row, who is scanning the gathering crowd of wedding guests as though looking for his wife to appear among them. To be married a lifetime, to make that pledge, and then to lose that person before life itself ends — this is a trick, a cruelty, like the flooding of a valley before everyone has left.

'Relax your shoulders,' she tells the group.

Of course, it's different depending on the couple. In her

parents' case, her mother would be freed if her father died first. But if her mother died, her father would be hopeless, would discard his cynicism about India and would wail at the feet of a golden statue after assigning his wife to the goddess of all injustice. Reema raises her arms in front of her, holding that imaginary ball before her chest, the way she was taught, giving them cues for their posture, but most of them look confused by this, so she drops her arms and turns to face their audience.

Jyoti and Aditya approach the platform hand in hand, Jyoti looking perfect in her shalwar kameez, no strings showing. Reema glances back at Monica, who is lining up her fellow altos so that they are even, shoulder to shoulder. The moon is becoming orange.

'You look gorgeous,' Jyoti says.

'You're joking ...' Reema manages to hold back from running her hand over her belly, and instead sweeps away the soft strand of hair that has escaped the bun at the top of her head.

'You all set?' Jyoti asks. Her voice has pops and cracks of misgiving, and Reema sees that even brides are uncertain of all they have. She would like to know just what it is that women are meant to be certain of.

'Anytime you are,' she says.

'Shame about Robert,' Jyoti says. 'He could have accompanied.' She strums her fingers at an air guitar, using the tone of voice she reserves for things uncouth. This tone is enough for Reema to miss Robert more than she can bear, regretting how his arms slackened around her as she told him she was going to the wedding alone.

'Let's sing, shall we?' Reema says, turning towards the choir. Will they remember the gestures she taught them at rehearsal? It will all be over soon enough in any case. One more day here, and she'll head north. At her family's planation she can rest and dream as she stares out over tea gardens. These cousins had been wise enough, long ago, to distrust the valley, to move to high land near Palampur.

'Smile,' she whispers to the choir. Monica is the first to part her lips, widen her mouth. The sounds will come, they will come what may. And the moon will tip over, giggling.

NINE

'You're sleepy,' she says, mostly to his chin which, at the angle he's holding his laptop, fills much of the screen. Skype is clear this morning, but Reema is whispering at the far side of the veranda, so that no one will hear. Breakfast plates are being assembled; the guests are in hammocks, in their rooms, or on poolside loungers. A pause in the festivities while omelettes are being prepared. The bulbul is preening and splashing on the surface of the pond that harbours the leaping fish — be careful, little bird.

'It's still dark here,' Robert says, opening his eyes wide to tease her for her early call. His growly voice is cheerful, with London inside it — Sundays on his sofa with football in the background of deep, dreamless naps.

'I tried to find a quiet moment.' The wedding guests are night owls; many of them are likely to miss breakfast again and will emerge at the height of the morning heat. Robert's hair is tousled, his chin shaded with stubble: he looks like he partied with the other guests last night, and for a moment she is jealous.

'How did the performance go?' he asks, but yawns, and this irritates her. She must try to stay on one feeling at a time.

'Fine,' she says. She gathers her hair up into a bun and ties a scrunchie around it. 'They came through. Impressive in the end, with a few screeches in the middle.'

'You're a pro,' he says, and moves closer to the camera. Her stomach lurches. There is always the surprise of him, always the same shock as that first night when she knew he wasn't like the men she was told by books or flighty girlfriends that she was supposed to love. 'I miss you,' she says.

'Me too.'

She swallows, feels her belly stir. Everything will be fine.

He says, 'Last night I was remembering a book we read in school, thinking of you there. Did you ever read Kipling's *Kim*?'

She sits back. Keep in mind he's making an effort; he's not a reader, and he can only know what he's been taught. But still she bristles as she did when they first met and he said, *I don't see your colour; I just see my kindred spirit.*

'How's work?' she says. His face hardens. 'What?' she says and sits back.

He is silent. She adjusts her blouse, pulling on the small lace hem so that the cotton covers her navel. She checks her face in the camera and smooths her eyebrow.

'You really want me to talk about work?'

His lips are pursed, thin. But he is so gentle.

'What do you mean?' She knows exactly what he means. The first argument they had was over her reluctance to meet his parents — too soon, too weighted — and he kept texting her to ask her to discuss it, to find out what was at the heart of her hesitation. She has always prided herself on doing what was asked of her, on being open, strong and available, taking anything that came her way. People on the street who ask for money, for food, for help. Her parents who ask for respect. But she is not *good*; she is just *curious*.

The right words would come if only she could pin down her feelings from one moment to another. Last year was simple. They had not stopped talking since the night in the bar, had been to films, concerts, dinners, and walks in Richmond Park, where they laughed like children and fell asleep under a tree. When he looked at her, she felt like part of him.

There is a tiny growth, like a skin tag but rounder and firmer, at the top of his thigh, so very near his testicles that it looks like a graft of one. When she first saw it, she touched it and startled him, making him self-conscious. She wasn't repulsed; she was frightened. For them. For their imperfections. She realises now that the flaw was so alive that it excited her. Alive in the way that death and life are perfectly superimposed.

'I need time,' she says.

'We don't have time.'

'We do, a bit longer,' she says, hoping that her careful accounting of the days is accurate, and that a decision will coincide with her return to London.

He shakes his head. There's a long silence between them.

'Why are you always wary of me? What have I ever done to make you wary?' he says.

There's a delay on the line; his movements are jerky like stop-motion photography. She says, 'I'm sorry, it's not that …' She leans closer to the screen.

'Let's speak when you've made up your mind,' he says.

Her first boyfriend, Jonathan, would have avoided conversation altogether, disappearing into his music. With him, she was the pursuer not the pursued. Maybe that's the difference between a musician and a man who works in advertising. A French horn player in his first year at the Royal College of Music, Jonathan needed to keep all the speech and breath and feeling between himself and his instrument. He broke her heart with his silence. But the secrets her mother told her as a girl are revealing themselves: there is a dance. One moment you are the person who loves more; the next you are the one running away.

'I will call you, promise,' she says.

———

Rum-drunk and holding tight on to a timber in the belly of the ship, 1941. Bananas being shipped from Caracas to Port of Spain, and we are stowaways. My artillery buddy's molasses voice in a whisper saying the Germans are too smart and careful of their torpedoes to sink a local schooner. But don't make a sound, Jackson, not even a fart. Just in case.

———

The lawn is unforgiving as she marches towards the lookout, searching the horizon of the reservoir. The cormorants will come. And leave. Cormorants have pattern and form and air to carry them.

She will scream again.

Two egrets fly to her right. Her sense of smell has become canine: there is something rotting in the garden. She turns and scans the lawn, trees, flower beds. Guests are scattered about, some early risers already in the stride of their day, returning from a morning meadow walk, or a paddle in a canoe. One man is doing furious lengths in the pool. The formalities of the wedding are behind them, and they have made themselves at home now. Jyoti is on the terrace pouring coffee for those who have arrived for breakfast. 'Thank you,' Jyoti says and laughs, *thank you*, over and over. She is a very good Indian wife now. Ankles, thighs, hips — all indentured. When she and Reema met in London as girls of fathers who had known each other in San Francisco, they were both rebellious and sad, both determined to kick arse in life, both striving to get into Mill Hill.

In Belmont Preparatory School and then at Mill Hill in north London, Jyoti and Reema boarded during the week and shared a room. Reema, on a music scholarship, worked hard to prove herself among posh English girls, and she progressed in music, English, and theatre. Jyoti, whose wealthy family had legacy in boarding schools in London, chose maths, biology and chemistry for her A-levels. One spring evening on the grass behind their dorm, as they were being taught to smoke by sixth formers, Reema had overheard Jyoti telling one of the girls that she would become a scientist and solve global warming.

Now she will live with this kind but bland man in a Delhi suburb?

'You always ruin everything …'

Reema turns towards the loud Irish accent to her left and sees a tall boxy man towering over a smaller, identical boxy boy of about ten.

'You never do what you're supposed to.'

Reema recognises the Irish man as the guest who clapped loudly and whistled when the choir ended their canon. His son is wearing shorts that knock his shins as he kicks pebbles in front of him.

'But I was going to do it,' the boy says, his face as hard as the man's.

'That's the thing with you,' says the father. He turns away, but doesn't walk off. 'You're always going to and you never do. You never do anything. Do what you're told — it's simple.' He turns back to face his son, who kicks extra-hard, pings a pebble at the wishing tree that has shed some of its wishes over the last two days. The slips of paper now lie under its branches like the wedding's autumn. The boy turns to walk away.

'Don't you walk away from me!'

The boy doesn't stop and the boxy man pursues him and grabs him by the shoulders with a force that whiplashes the child's head. The boy's hands go to his neck.

'I don't want to be around you,' the boy says.

'Oh, you don't, do you? You have ruined my entire holiday. You always do. You have ruined everything.'

They walk in opposite directions, the boy kicking pebbles and grass.

Reema heads for the lookout. Come, monkey.

——

On the terrace, the queue for the breakfast buffet is building. Reema searches for Monica. Monica with lists and places to visit, Monica who has lost her job in the crash but is nevertheless on a holiday, Monica who sings out of tune with a smile. She spots her.

'Want to come with me to Pune?' she says, as she arrives by Monica's side in the queue. This has come out of nowhere except a memory that Pune is good for music. In her careful calculations, she could skip her cousin and the tea plantation, take a short flight to have an adventure, and still be within the safe limit. Monica is the perfect tourist, and as two women together in the south they'll be safe, while Reema learns Dhrupad music and how to sing from her thighs. Monica holds an empty plate with a bowl rested on top of it, eyeing the offerings on the breakfast buffet. As she turns to Reema with a questioning look, Yosh arrives behind them.

'Your concert was beautiful,' he says to Reema. She looks into his angled face. He is wearing glasses.

'All down to the singers,' Reema says, and points to Monica.

'You haven't joined us in the mornings,' Yosh says, his head a see-saw of politeness.

'I'm not bendy,' Reema says.

There's a moment of silence that amuses itself with the word *bendy*, and she becomes embarrassed.

'You don't have to be bendy at first,' Monica says. She moves a little closer, and Reema watches her slouch slightly next to Yosh, the way a tall woman sometimes will around a man she is attracted to.

'It's not only a physical practice,' Yosh adds.

Reema moves along in the queue. She's not hungry, but she must eat something. Monica is a friendly name. If Reema's father had not decided he wanted to become a real Indian and had stayed in San Francisco might Reema have been born at all? And if she had, might her name have been Scarlett, Madison, Olivia, Chloe, or Ashley?

'Is this the limit of your trip?' Yosh asks Reema as they step forward in the queue.

'Pune,' Monica answers for her.

Yosh looks surprised. 'It's a long way to the south,' he says. 'Have you been farther north?'

His face is stern, as though what she's considering is unreasonable, and of course it is. She says, 'It was just a thought. I also have family in Palampur who are expecting me.'

'Yosh has agreed to be my guide,' Monica says, making it clear she won't be joining Reema in Pune.

'We are headed north today,' Yosh says. He glances at Monica but doesn't wait for her approval. 'You could join us.'

Reema takes a fork, knife, a napkin. She senses a reaction in Monica. Glancing towards the lookout, Reema searches for the egrets. Acacia leaves stir; she does miss him. Choices are sharp, but also thick.

'I don't want to intrude,' she says.

'It's not far from Dharmsala, not even an hour. Do you know Dharamkot?' Yosh says. He holds her inside the question.

Reema waits to see if time will stand still. Time *can* stand still. People are wrong about this. She has felt it before: when she's singing, when she and Robert embrace, in spring when she stands under the magnolia tree outside her flat in Kilburn before entering it, and pretends that the flat is bigger than it really is. She catches Yosh's eye, but he looks towards the buffet ahead of them. Only now does Reema notice the words on Monica's T-shirt. *I'm in it for the shavasana*. The first time she saw a shirt like this in London she was confused about its meaning, but Robert explained it — Robert, who has never been to a yoga class in his life, but who knows slogans and T-shirts and the brilliance of putting words together.

Shavasana is the corpse pose. Yosh must offer this at the end of each session. What must it be like to offer bodies the feeling of a corpse? 'Nothing to do, nothing to be: shavasana ...' her yoga teacher had said. Strangers lying down together to feel the end. And the end is something to look forward to.

'Yes, I'd like to come,' she says.

When Reema checks the look on Monica's face she can't be sure of anything. She reaches the food laid out in large, delicate ceramic bowls. The yoghurt will make her nauseous, but she might be able to manage toast.

'After Dharmsala we'll go east, to Manali, then south to Shimla and back to Kangra, a circle,' Yosh says.

'Like Siddhartha's,' Monica says. Reema notices Yosh's shoulders rise.

She wonders what *the real thing* is that Mike referred to, and how it might be possible to earn a living and be real at the same time. Yosh would never be a teacher who would yell, at a room of fifteen women with blonde ponytails, *find peace where there is no peace*. Next to her he spoons papaya and mango into a bowl. The morning has become hotter. 'We could detour to Palampur on the way back,' he adds.

Reema slices some bread for the toaster. 'How long will you be up there?' She adds up days in her mind, balances the ledger of travel with what the clinic told her.

Yosh looks at Monica. 'Open-ended, I think — up to you.'

Monica nods, but her face has hardened. Still she says, 'Yes, great. Come along.'

Reema waits for time to stop again, but this you cannot force. Yosh's hair is thick and straight like a mare's tail. His shoulders are soft, broad, arms sculpted but not pumped. Beside Robert he would be a similar height. She thinks of Jackson, how shrunken he seems. Maybe love shrinks you.

'I'll see if I can drag someone else along, to balance things out,' she says, trying to reassure Monica.

'Leaving around three,' Monica says, offering a smile.

Monica reminds her of a girl at school, the one who helped everyone with their exams. While Reema could remember the position of notes on a stave, this girl knew everything else. At the ponds on Hampstead Heath, the swans were fat. One had a crooked neck. Her classmates were silly about the swan. *Genus cygnus curvus crassus* the clever girl said, and the others laughed because the girl knew how to say fat in Latin. This was what school required of them: to memorise the names of things — parallelogram, trapezium, the Magna Carta, the War of the Roses, stratus, cirrus, nimbus, cumulus — but never the sound of things, or the right way for people to treat one another.

'Okay,' Reema says. *Accha*. She takes her piece of toast from the toaster as she lays her plate back in the pile. She heads to the other side of the terrace. Perhaps Yosh will teach her how to squat, and if crown, shoulders, arms must pass through, she will be balanced on her heels, crouched in malasana.

———

She hears the old man's voice telling jokes in a circle of Jyoti's relatives. She watches as each of them nod at every word, take him in with their eyes as though he is something to behold, not just an old man, and for this too she is grateful for India and ashamed of her father who considered putting her granny in a home rather than bringing her from California to live with them. In the time it took for him to decide, she collapsed and died at a neighbour's front door in Fremont.

Jackson stands up and excuses himself, making another joke, this one about the risks of delaying the call of nature at his age. She follows him.

She waits at the foot of the small stairs that lead to his room. A dried stain of civet cat blood on the stones catches her eye. She stares into it. When she finishes her teacher training in England, she could return to Delhi, learn to speak Hindi properly. Teaching could take her anywhere. Europe. In Germany, singers are well paid. Or in London she could use both of her musical traditions; she could break new ground, do a Master's at the Royal College, the place where she first lost confidence.

One morning she'd arrived to surprise Jonathan in his dorm. As she thinks now of the cat hair she found on his black suit, the day after his first Royal College orchestra appearance and the late night he had spent with his mates, the pain resurfaces. The flautist had talked often of her new kitten. The white hairs on her sofa had transferred to his suit — the base of the trouser legs, the seam at the crotch, and there, even on the rayon lining of the back pocket, suggesting they had been taken off and turned inside out. The laconic Jonathan didn't have to say a word to Reema after that morning, which was just as well for both of them. Love and white cat hairs. And an ache to bury.

'Penny for your thoughts,' Jackson says. She looks up into his smile as he comes towards her down the stairs.

'Excuse me,' she says.

'For what?' He stops in his descent.

She looks behind her. The rotting smell from the other side of the garden has made its way over.

'A young person like you doesn't need to be excused,' he says, and continues down the steps to her. 'But someone needs to do something about Mike's chilli omelette.' He chuckles. She feels lighter.

'Would you like to go up north?' she says. He cocks his head. The sun is warm on her shoulder. She pushes her hair behind her ear. 'I thought maybe you'd like a bit of a road trip. Monica has hired Yosh to take us to the mountains.'

Jackson straightens up and tries to remember what month it was, which year, where they had been living when he and Amelia were in the Himalayas together. It's an option he hadn't considered.

'Interesting thought,' he says. Amelia loved the snow, loved the window-sill-high piles of it in their front yard in Boston. Once as they learned to cross-country ski at a Berkshire resort, both of them in their sixties with time and a bit of energy left, she said, as the snow glittered, the sun nearly blinding them, 'We could lie down here and sleep. It would be one way to go before the indignities begin. Freezing and drowning are supposed to be the easiest, and they'd only find us once the snow melted.' When he laughed and agreed with her, it felt like a pact, which was as much of one as they'd ever had on the subject. So why not take her to the snow and then just lie down and be done with it.

'Do you want to think about it? I'll come back with more details once I have them,' Reema says.

'Yes, good,' he says. She touches his arm like someone on the same team, like a comrade in arms, and leaves him.

———

I hug the rifle against my shoulder, step in line with the Venezuelan boys who want to go to war, but their country insists they are neutral, their country has brought minesweepers from Fascist Italy and a coastguard from the Americans to protect their oil, and while my brother is away at university and I have no one to talk with of war, I volunteer with the artillery and parade in Caracas with a rifle, like playing capture the flag with boys on the streets of Calgary.

TEN

Timing is everything. Jackson makes his way along the outer perimeter of the garden and wonders why he hadn't considered the snow before. He could have stayed in Boston. But there are no coincidences. This opportunity, up there where he and Amelia had once trekked, could be just the thing, and Yosh just the man to get him there.

In Boston, after he'd retired but when he still taught the engineering foundation course at the community college, Jackson had met a young man from India who pronounced *w* and *v* with no distinction and rolled *r*s on his tongue. *Vhat I know about the rrest of the vorld vould fit on this page,* he told Jackson in his first tutorial in fluid mechanics, holding up a blank sheet ripped from a notebook. No one ever corrected his pronunciation, and no one at the college except Jackson knew that the man had probably come to America with nothing but a desire to escape his caste. But Jackson understood a thing or two more than his fellow instructors. He told them to keep an eye out, pay special attention. In winter the Indian student had arrived to lectures with soaking feet and a terrified glare; by the spring, he was getting the highest grades in the class. Amelia asked Jackson to invite him for dinner. It didn't seem appropriate, so he never did, but now there is Yosh. He is a young man whom Amelia would have taken to immediately for his gentle manner, his clear eyes. This young man understands something about getting ahead in the world, his accent carefully managed. But he does yoga not business; this contradiction is curious. Jackson knocks on Yosh's door.

When Yosh opens it, it's clear that Jackson has disturbed him. There's a cushion on the floor in front of a candle, and Yosh is in a thin singlet and shorts.

'I hope I'm not interrupting,' Jackson says.

'Not at all,' he says with a nod, even more now like the fluid mechanics student. 'Please come in.'

As Yosh turns and walks back into his room, Jackson notices finger-like scars on his back, fanning out from beneath the singlet towards his shoulder. Yosh offers Jackson the armchair and sits on the edge of the bed.

Jackson sits down. 'Reema says you are going to the mountains.'

'Yes, later today.'

'Do you have family there?' Jackson looks about the room, taking in the careful details of colour, the knick-knacks of Northern Indian culture. But, of course, this is not the man's home.

'No.'

The room smells of mornings in the administrative office at the dam site, incense and perspiration. Jackson knows the smell of men at work. Binoculars, leather-bound ledgers, draughting pens and measuring rods ... Suddenly he doesn't remember why he's come.

'Mr Baines?'

'Where do you live in Vancouver?' Jackson asks.

Yosh looks around the room as though for a way out, then clears his throat. 'Eastside.'

'I was there for a few weeks once, for business. In the summer, though.' He can't remember the project specifically, but he can picture the Vancouver office of the engineers there who had hired him as a consultant. 'Do you get much snow in winter?'

'More rain than snow.'

'Do you like the snow?'

There are people Jackson knows in Victoria, where Amelia's sister lives. For a man to progress, he needs to know the right people. Jackson had discipline and contacts; his brother had good luck. Ashok Parmar — the Dalit millionaire with the two pens — must have had both, as well as strength. The young student in Boston with the fused ws and vs had sheer determination. This young man has something different altogether — control over his body. He might just need a contact and a decent break. Victoria is a city with potential. Amelia's sister never liked Jackson for taking her sister farther away with each job he secured; he doesn't know her two daughters, from whom he's not heard a word since the funeral. But they might help Yosh. At Tofino, on Long Beach, Jackson had stood on a rock by the shore and let the spray of the Pacific salt his lips.

'I am amused by the snow,' Yosh says. 'It always surprises me.'

'I might still know people in business in BC — you could look them up, they could be of help,' Jackson says, but is worried he will never remember their names.

'You think I need help?' Yosh says, dryly.

Jackson didn't mean to offend. Perhaps he has made a mistake by considering Reema's offer to go north with them.

Amritsar is a holy place they tell me, and I am taken with the turbaned men who welcome me to one of the five sarovars of the city. They are kind. They show me how they bathe there, but I do not join them. I am ashamed as I watch the men together in the water.

Jackson steadies himself. 'The snow is different in the mountains,' he says and waves in the general direction of the Himalayas. 'Mountain snow is tougher, and more beautiful.'

'Yes, you are right,' Yosh says. There is a long silence. 'And thank you for your offer.'

There is something in these young people he can't quite put his finger on. Jackson feels the dark edge again, and he dares not imagine what it is that makes them sometimes unpleasant.

Yosh stands, as if to say *please get on with what you want from me*, so Jackson stands too. As Yosh turns his back to Jackson and folds up maps and places his binoculars in the suitcase, Jackson becomes concerned. The feathered scars are like marks from a whip, keloid fingerprints.

'But Canada is not as spiritual as India,' Jackson says.

Yosh glances at him, over his shoulder, then puts a few more things into his suitcase, silently. 'People think India is spiritual,' he says eventually. 'It is and it is not. It is many things, including the opposite of spiritual.'

Jackson closes his eyes. *There are people in the street, a man comes beside him.* He opens his eyes quickly.

'What happened to your back?' he says.

Yosh sits on the bed. 'Was there something specific you came for?'

'I wonder if you might take me with you,' Jackson says. 'I will pay my fair share.'

The young man bristles, but says, 'Of course, you're welcome to come. With Reema.'

Reema's name has a special intonation in Yosh's mouth.

'I'd like to see the snow.'

'You are welcome to come,' Yosh says.

He and Amelia had an argument when he failed to bring the Indian student home for dinner. She told him he had to discover people by talking to them, but that all he ever did was talk *at* them. This he must remember. As he leaves the room, he has to shield his eyes from the brightness of the sun.

ELEVEN

As the Maharana Pratap Sagar reservoir recedes behind them, the road becomes steeper, embedded in the cliffs that have been carved out of the mountain. The hired Tata SUV veers left, right, and left again, following the road's curves, and Reema holds the handle above the door as she studies the ochre swirls of stone embedded in the mountain wall. This stone was also what lined the shore of the reservoir. Beside her in the back seat, Jackson remembers his geography lessons. He knows the origins of the Himalayas: they were once beneath the Tethys Sea. Under the sea, a mountain takes its time to grow.

Reema feels the pitch of the road in her legs, her groin, her belly, and she tightens the seat belt across her lap. The peaks of the mountains are close, like neighbouring hills, not framed like a postcard as they were from the meadow. And the road is rough. She looks at the back of Yosh's head, then beside it through the front windscreen, and finally beyond Monica in the passenger seat, as she tries to hold a fixed point on the horizon. The fan of the air conditioning is a riot of wings inside the jeep.

Yosh glances in the rear-view mirror and she catches his eye. He looks quickly back at the road and presses the play button on the console. Bhangra music pours out too loudly; he reaches for the volume, turns it down low. Reema touches her forehead where there are small beads of sweat.

'We'll start with Masroor Temple,' Yosh says and looks at her again in the mirror.

Reema feels a vinegary bile in her throat, swallows it back.

'... made by Pandavas, and dedicated to Rama, Lakshman and Sita ...'

She pushes the door open on a slow curve and vomits bile and tea.

'You're ill!' Jackson puts his hand on her shoulder.

Reema sits back and pulls the door shut, glances up front to see Monica's shocked face.

'It's nothing,' Reema says, wiping her mouth. 'Just carsick.'

The car veers to the side of the road, but there is not enough space for it to stop on the shoulder, and beyond it is a steep drop. 'Hold on,' Yosh says and puts the car gently in motion, as though it is made of glass.

'It's nothing,' Reema says again.

Jackson touches her hand, but she steels herself and holds her gaze on the horizon. He fetches the water bottle from the floor of the car and hands it to her. She shakes her head.

'I'm sorry,' Yosh says, 'the road ...' and she feels the car pull off onto the gravel shoulder. She looks at Monica, who rummages through her handbag. Reema closes her eyes.

'You should sit up front if you get carsick,' Yosh says.

No, she thinks, as she opens her eyes to see Monica holding out some mints. Then Monica's face falls as she lowers her hand. She pops out one mint from its pack and puts it in her mouth before she opens the passenger door to get out.

As the exchange takes place, Jackson sneaks a look at his

suitcase. Amelia, bear with them. They are young; it's normal to have a commotion.

———

Elephants. A few in a line, head to tail, one following the other; some solitary elephants, others in herds, still others accompanying armies. These lines carved in rock are worn and yet so precise that Jackson can almost feel their hides. He touches the wall of the Masroor temple, which Yosh tells him is one of the oldest in the Kangra valley.

Cut out of free-standing rock, the walls are carved altars with framed pedestals for Ram, Lakshman and Sita. As Yosh explains how rock-cut temples are more difficult for the artists because the shape is determined by what is already there, rather than by the imagination, Jackson fans his face with his hand and says, *oh, please, not now,* to his bladder. The group moves among the temple carvings, running their hands over the shapes on the walls. There is a chai seller with a stall to their left. Jackson watches as the middle-aged man sets a pot on a grate over a gas cylinder and then stands staring into space, as he must do day upon day.

In those early years of their marriage, as Jackson and Amelia travelled by train in the north and dipped down to the centre of India, they visited many temples like this. Madhya Pradesh — the Khajuraho temples, with their elephants at war, their nymphs in anklets caught in the moment of stripping off diaphanous saris or straddling a male. Couples depicted in intercourse, while attendants assist and fondle, partaking in the coupling: small orgies of entry, back and front, upside down, male and female in equal pleasure. Amelia stood among them, entranced. She told him that life in the west was limited and stale, that he should take note, that life was short and they must make the most of it. The sculptures aroused yet embarrassed him, the stiff penises of the men that entered horses as well as females.

This temple, Yosh says, was built in the eighth century. He points to a man and woman entwined in the rock face. Yaksha and Yakshi, he tells them. Jackson watches Yosh's expression; he seems to disdain the very things he's describing, as though these gods are connivers, as though he has to struggle to share this knowledge, is hired to do so, but believes none of it. Yosh's eyes take in Reema's shoulders from time to time, and move to her long, shapely arms. Everywhere there are breasts and elephants and Jackson must be vigilant on Reema's behalf.

An Indian lawyer, Yosh says, has recently filed a case in Bihar against the Hindu god Lord Ram over alleged mistreatment of his wife Sita, citing Ram's brother, Lakshman, as a conspirator in renouncing Sita.

'They filed a lawsuit against a god?' Monica says.

Yosh nods in agreement at the absurdity. He explains that Lord Ram banished Sita to live in exile in a forest and the lawyer claims the move was cruel and hypocritical treatment. Reema watches Yosh as he touches the wall with Yaksha and Yakshi. She senses that by unfolding these stories he is earning his fee. But he is like her father in these matters, distrusting of any belief for which a statue has to be sculpted.

Looking up to the outer edges of the temple grounds, Reema

sees three young men sitting on rubble, watching them. One of them wears shoes; the other two have strips of dungaree tied around their feet.

Yosh leads them deeper into the temple grounds. She wanders among the stone carvings, stares at the head of Buddha and the six-headed god holding a weapon, riding on top of what looks like a peacock. She is no longer using *accha* in her thoughts. There is no way in which she could fake her belonging here.

'I didn't know there were elephants this far north,' Jackson says, coming up beside her. 'They could have had one at the wedding.' She doesn't catch the joke, not interested. 'It's quite hot,' he adds, because of course a young woman could care less about relic carvings; a young woman should be, what? Dancing. Making the world bow to her energy like the S-curved Devi in her dance, as though saying *make way for me*. 'There's dancing,' he says as he points to the likeness of Devi.

Reema holds her hand out to touch the carving. 'My mother showed me things like these as a child,' she says, 'but I was having none of it.' When Sadhana, her teacher, taught her to sing *sa*, the peacock, she held her arm up like this carving, made her body a snake, not a peacock.

'I began to learn Urdu when I was an intern in the Punjab, many years ago. Just a young fella. After Partition and before I met Amelia. I had a room in a guest house in Amritsar, run by a Parsi woman.' He doesn't have to try to remember her name, but he pauses nonetheless. Her face has come to mind from time to time, these past sixty years. She had been the first woman in the Punjab to drive a car, then to own one, a woman far ahead of her time. 'Mrs

Bhandari,' he says. He closes his eyes. It's so hot today. He wonders what became of Mrs Bhandari, if she's still alive, if she's stopped driving. What if he could drive himself to Amritsar to see her?

'Refugee nonsense,' railed the engineer at the sight of Mrs Bhandari bent over reams of cloth as she worked through the night stitching garments for the half-clad children who crossed into the city, and I saw his sneer and I saw his Rolex watch and there was war raging across the border between Pakistan and Kashmir. I was learning from Guldasta, her nickname, but oh, the engineer complained and grinned.

The temple terracotta is cracked and dry before him when he opens his eyes again. 'I don't have much time,' he says.

She steps towards him urgently but sees that he looks well. 'Do you mean for what is in your suitcase?' she says, realising.

'I need to decide,' he says. 'Why not here?'

She surveys the area: rock walls with bodies carved into them, the ochre deepening at the foot of the temples where untouched by the sun. The small pond is stagnant, mossy, and as green as a meadow. Come, little fish. Why not? Why not here for the old man's wife?

'It could be very peaceful here. There aren't many tourists,' she says.

Jackson makes a fist while he considers it.

She sashays like a model on her cross-country skis, I slip and slide behind her to catch up and forty years disappear as the snow blinds me, the sky becomes Panama and I say wait, I want to tell you about wooden ponies, lawns with swings, rubber inner tubes in rivers, train sets, coos and whispers at night and the unfathomable ways a man can be jealous, wait ...

'I think I would like to go higher up, into the mountains,' he says, but Reema is not listening. She is looking towards the fence.

He glances over to see the three men lined up, dishevelled, like tired soldiers fronting a barricade.

Reema watches the young men, while Jackson watches her.

One of them is smiling, another is talking, as though to himself, but his voice is deep and coaxing. Her father always told her that to have strength you needed nothing more than a sense of your own voice. But these men hold power by being shoulder to shoulder: stronger together. Softly, softly, we must go in life, her father would say. But these men standing by the fence are not going softly. The third man searches the ground, sweeps rubble aside with his feet. She turns to Jackson.

'Did your wife like the mountains?'

'She liked the snow,' he says. 'I'd like to take her to the snow.'

Reema looks up towards the mountain range, to see how possible this might be. The peaks are iced like a dessert. She doesn't know anything about snow or roads to snow; in London it comes every few years and creates havoc. 'That sounds like a good idea,' she says.

'We should move on,' Yosh says, arriving beside them. 'We would like daylight when we arrive in Dharamsala.' He gestures for them to follow him. Reema looks around for Monica, who is on the other side of the pond, too close, she thinks, to the young men by the fence. Yosh waves to get Monica's attention, but she doesn't see him.

'I'll get her,' Reema says.

As she walks across the temple grounds the sun on her shoulder is intense. Monica seems more exposed there beside the pond, taking photos from different angles.

'We're going,' she calls. Monica lowers her camera and waits for Reema to reach her. 'Yosh said I should get you.'

'It looks like Stonehenge,' Monica says. Reema turns to take in this perspective of the pillars of the temple. 'Or chess pieces,' Monica adds. 'I wonder if there is an Indian chess set.'

'What do you mean?'

'I need some gifts to take home.'

Reema hasn't considered gifts for Robert, for her parents.

'No one knows I lost my job. They'll be expecting them,' Monica says.

'We need to go.'

'I learned a mantra once, to Krishna, goes like *Vamshee vibhooshita karaan navaneeradaabhaat. Peetaambaraadaruna bimbaphalaa dharoshthaat …*'

They laugh. Monica really is just like that clever girl from school.

'My family won't understand,' Monica says, looking to her for approval. They share a moment opposite to the ones she's had with Jackson. This moment is fluid and slippery, and aware of all the things that don't matter anyway.

The only thing to understand is the absolute nonsense of things. *Ridiculous* would be the word she would borrow from Robert. One month you can have everything; the next month you fling yourself from a skyscraper. She worries about her brother. He has told her that things are bad now in the States, burying her with new stories and statistics every time they speak. He is obsessed with imminent danger. A financial analyst threw himself out of the window of his twenty-ninth-floor apartment in New Jersey; a real estate broker blew his head off at a wildlife reserve; a twenty-three-year-old woman from Pennsylvania robbed a bank to pay her rent; and a woman in Georgia, who instead of going to court for her eviction hearing, called the police to warn them that she was about to take her own life. It was too late when they arrived at the apartment: she had chosen to die rather than leave a place she couldn't afford. When Reema objected to his regular barrage of fatalities, her brother hit her with one last story: about the twenty-four-year-old man from Milwaukee, fired three weeks previously, who had suffocated himself with cellophane.

She reaches for Monica's shoulder and brushes off a small leaf that has landed there. 'You'll get another one ...'

There's a hiss to their right, at first like an animal's, but no. Reema adjusts the straps of her tank top. More sounds, rustling and laughter.

'You fuck me,' calls one of the young men. The others hoot, laugh.

'You fuck me,' he calls again, to the same response from his friends.

Monica and Reema quickly turn in the opposite direction, heading around the back of the pond. When they finally reach Yosh, neither of them mentions the men; something hangs between her and Monica like smoke from a joint shared in secret. The shame that *you fuck me* could have been their fault. But now the men are hooting loudly.

'We're going,' Yosh says, and she and Monica follow him. She glances back to see that the young men have disappeared.

When they reach the carvings of Yakshi and Yaksha where they left Jackson, he is nowhere to be found. 'I'll see if he's around the other side,' Yosh says, and he and Monica leave Reema to wait for Jackson in the shelf of shade provided by the temple.

Jackson zips up his fly, relieved he's been left alone to go about his business in a corner out of sight of the others. 'My apologies, sir,' he says with a salute to the stone elephant as he leaves. He sees Reema, waiting for him by the first temple tower. Sweat drips from his chin to the collar of his shirt as he walks with purpose towards her. There's nothing like Indian temperatures, Amelia, you remember that. Nothing like plains and hillsides and the dust when the heat is like dry steam. He quickens his step. The light emanating from the rock walls is nearly pink. In Boston there is snow that turns green a few days after the pissing dogs have marked their territory. The snow in the mountains will be just the thing. He hears a noise and looks up towards the top of the temple.

A golf-ball-sized stone strikes his forehead above his right eye.

There's a whooping call from the top of the rock. The voices of the three young men blend with the sound of a scattering of stones. Footfalls. A shower of pebbles. Some lodge in his hair; others fall to his shoulders.

'Oh my god!' Reema says, running towards him. Jackson's legs have folded beneath him with the blow. He holds his head; blood seeps between his fingers. 'Are you all right?' She kneels, opens her pack and fetches tissues.

She moves his hand away and examines the small gash across his eyebrow where blood drips towards his eye. Looking around for Yosh, she sees him at the temple wall holding on to a horizontal bar of the scaffolding that has been erected for temple repairs. He pulls himself up, climbing the rungs, reaching a platform towards the top of the temple. He calls out in a dialect, threatening. Somehow he knows how to speak to the men running away with their dungaree-wrapped feet and rope belts loose and falling. He backs down the scaffolding and runs towards the entrance to the temple grounds.

'I'll call the police,' he shouts to Reema and Jackson.

Reema holds a tissue under Jackson's cut, but the blood soaks through it. She unfurls the sheer scarf from her pack and hands it to him. Jackson hesitates, shaking his head, but she insists. He takes it and presses it to the cut over his eye. The blood trickles. Reema watches him, one hand raised ready to take over from him. His face seems suddenly younger.

The chai seller brings cups of tea on a small silver tray, and places the tray on the ground beside them. He speaks to them in an urgent and apologetic voice, pointing and complaining, then retreats. Jackson looks into Reema's face, worried that he has lost his sense of smell — no jasmine, cardamom, or nutmeg coming from her.

'Did you see them?' he asks her. She hands him a cup of tea and looks back towards the temple. The driver for the few other visitors to the temple ushers his clients towards their mini-van.

'Not throwing the stones, no,' she says, putting down the chai, and leans forward to take the hand in which he holds the scarf. She pulls his hand away; the blood still trickles. Taking over from him, she presses down on his brow. She draws out another tissue with her free hand and catches some blood that is about to drip into his eye. A bird caws loudly behind them.

'It's still bleeding,' she says. 'I'll press harder?'

'It's the warfarin,' he says, but she doesn't understand. 'Makes the blood thin. Clotting will take some time.'

She looks around for Yosh and Monica but can't see them. There is no breeze as she continues to press the scarf against his brow.

'They're just boys,' Jackson says.

She notices that his chest is rising and falling quickly. 'Are you thirsty?' she asks, nodding at the cup in his hand.

'No,' he says, 'I'm never thirsty enough. Amelia always said, drink, drink!' Feeling blood, he wipes his cheek and takes one sip. 'I'll be fine,' he says.

She looks towards the top of the temple, almost expecting that the young men might appear. More birds caw, but then there is nothing for a long time: no rustling, no sound, and the pink light from the temple seems to fade.

'We're a long way from home,' she says.

The trick with young children, she's learned from teaching, is to distract them. A child who has an injury and is crying becomes a child who would like to learn about a lion with a thorn in its paw. 'Did your wife know India too?' she says.

He takes in her face again — elegant, not dangerous; he doesn't know what all the dread was about. 'She loved it,' he says. But he's not entirely sure this is the truth. Amelia loved the spice, the textiles, the food, the music, but did Amelia love India?

'Even the chaos?' she asks. English people always mention the chaos of Delhi, but she has no sense that it was chaos she was born into. Life before memory is a cocoon of other people's stories, punctuated by a vague soundtrack of voices, cooing, whispering, praying for a baby who will make everyone proud.

'She loved it,' Jackson says. Again, he wonders. Amelia liked the household ordered, the table set a particular way, a schedule for laundry and cleaning. He remembers the tone of her voice once, to a housekeeper they employed in Jalna ... *How dare you?* ... when the woman smelled of Amelia's perfume. Jackson skulked down the hallway pretending not to have heard. 'She was perfect,' he tells Reema, quickly, then removes Reema's hand from his forehead to check how much blood has soaked her scarf.

'Yes, I can imagine,' Reema says.

She has had men tell her about perfection — the shape and colour of her eyes, the length and curve of her legs. The way she speaks, the fullness of her lips. Her pleasant manner. Not Robert, though. Robert rarely mentions her beauty. He hones in on her determination. Robert is a man who believes that if you work hard, freedom will come. He appreciates that she has ambition, but thinks she's certainly far from perfect.

'You should see the rest of your country,' Jackson says.

'Yes, I know.'

'Amritsar,' he says eagerly, but that city might not be right for her. The unsavoury history — a shot into a crowd of protesters, the mob killing of an English teacher, the British colonel who forced Indians to crawl on hands and knees, the protest in the garden of Jallianwala Bagh, the colonel's order for machine-gun fire, the numbers of dead that weren't tallied. Decades later, the raid on the Golden Temple was supported by Thatcher. He'd rather not discuss this.

'Mrs Bhandari made fine tea, always put the milk in first, believing that was how a white person would prefer it.' He takes a deep breath.

'There now,' Reema says, pressing the scarf against his eyebrow again.

'Each day I travelled by rickshaw to the dam offices. But there was a war nearby — new Pakistan and old India — and there was so much ...' he stops. 'It was very different then.'

The minivan engine revs, and the driver leans on the horn as though to scare someone or something out of the way.

'There are other places to see, as well,' he adds.

She nods. Her family never returned to India together. Her mother grieves silently, has come alone just a few times. Her brother has come for business. But her father had never been back, and this has been Reema's first trip since she was a baby.

She says, 'My father told me that the Taj Mahal was not real — that it was a movie set for romantic films and that the only people there were extras. He has something against this country.'

Several minutes pass when it seems that nothing special has happened at all, except for the trickles of blood at Jackson's temple.

The air stirs and he can smell Reema's clothes again. Coconut oil, grass, tree bark. He is relieved. The breeze swells. The minivan pulls out. The bird caws loudly again and again.

'This is good,' he says.

'What's good?'

'Now. This. It's good.'

She puts her chai back on the silver tray and takes the bent fingers of his right hand. She rubs them, staring at the age spots near his knuckles and thinking that he might have been handsome as a young man, despite the small stature; old people shrink. There is an elegance about him that men her age don't seem to have. When does that take hold? Who is this Mrs Bhandari in Amritsar who makes a light come on in him?

'The guard has called the police,' Yosh says, and Reema looks up to see him stop short, as though sensing he might be interrupting something.

'And maybe a doctor?' she says, waving him closer. Yosh approaches and sits down beside them.

'Those boys were just playing,' Jackson says.

She and Yosh exchange a knowing look.

'Where's Monica?' she asks.

'In the jeep,' Yosh says. 'Are you fine, Mr Baines?'

'Absolutely. They're just boys,' Jackson says.

Yosh crosses his legs. 'Yes, maybe,' he says.

Reema watches as he prepares to say more. It comes out slowly, as though he's hesitant to make a point that will offend them. He says that with tourists this kind of thing usually never happens, and he's sorry. Maybe it's his fault, maybe he shouldn't have brought them here, but in some ways it's not a surprise. Boys, like these, he says, they are angry. In his tone he is searching for a kind way to explain.

'A few years ago, one June, I and two friends trekked from Manali to Bhrigu Lake, crossing snow, right up on top of the world,' he says.

Reema watches his forehead crease in thought. This makes him look older.

'We had a lot of trouble with the local boys. They despised us. We think they spit in our chai before handing it to us.'

Jackson fidgets, tries to get more comfortable on the ground.

His knee hurts and his feet have let him down again. He takes over from Reema now, pressing the scarf against his wound.

'I think they were right to despise us,' Yosh says.

'Please,' Jackson says suddenly to Reema, and raises his hand to indicate he'd like to stand.

Both Reema and Yosh rush to help him to his feet. Reema brushes the dirt and pebbles from his trouser legs.

'I'm fine, I'm fine,' Jackson says and shakes off their hands.

Reema steps back and lets Jackson steady himself. Some young men are running away with feet wrapped in dungaree cloth; others are throwing themselves from skyscrapers.

'India isn't what people always think it is,' Yosh says, and Jackson wonders why he feels he must repeat this perspective for him as though he's an old man who does not listen the first time.

TWELVE

In Gaggal, the mountains are closer, the peaks white: Jackson will be pleased. Reema watches him from across the road, sitting at the chai stall where they left him. He looks left and right, up then down, shifts on his chair, taps his foot, touches the bandage on his forehead, looks into his lap. Hopefully he is not in pain.

The petrol station to her left is newly built; there is an ATM and a travel agency where the internet is available. This is a town with purpose. The travel agent has just told her the new airport, a few miles away, is making all the difference, his face moist with thoughts of all the business it will bring him.

She fondles the brochure for Pune in her hand. It's still possible to escape. By plane, or somewhere else by train. She's not responsible for Jackson. Time can stand still.

A village man in a muslin turban leads horses on a rope down the main street past her. They are slow and placid, following along without energy. She counts seven in total: five fully grown horses and two foals. Open your eyes, little horse.

In the toilet of the petrol station she'd examined her face in the small cracked mirror that hung over the dirt-smeared sink. Her cheeks are fuller, her eyes puffy. In Pune she would know no one, and the travel agent said that women travel alone to the music festival there, more Dhrupad musicians are women, and the oldest

Hindustani music in the culture is getting an upgrade. She wanted to believe him. The slow slides and monotones of a raag in a woman's voice would bring ... something.

She delays crossing back over the road to Jackson's side. Yosh is doing the kind of errand he has done when they've made stops — she's not sure what — and Monica is taking photos. Wandering into the shop next to the petrol station, she is met by rows and rows of sewing machines. Black Singer machines from the 1950s, with foot pumps and the Singer logo in bright gold capitals. Later models, electric machines with hand wheels and bobbin threaders, higher up on a shelf. Thimbles, thread, scissors. The shop is a museum of tailoring through several decades. She turns the hand wheel of one of the machines, making the needle go up and down, thinking of Jackson seated alone at a table by the road. He has given the police a statement, has seen a doctor who cleaned the wound that ended up being smaller than they had thought, and has been pronounced fit to carry on. If she could, she'd cut one of the horses loose from the others, mount it, ride out of town, encourage it to gallop through the valley, to pause by a river to drink, to climb up and down gentle hills and be eyed from above by eagles.

She leaves the sewing machines and returns to the road. A cow walks beside her and cuts in front, having spotted something to graze on a little farther ahead. Cyclists ring their bells and wind around the cow, through the people, the cars. She sees Monica farther up, near the man in the muslin turban and his horses. Monica raises her camera to take photographs. Run, little horse.

———

At the chai stall a young boy serves tea as Jackson takes in the boy's asymmetry. Carrying everything in his left hand only, the boy holds the stump of his right wrist against the pot to steady it. Jackson looks up to see the boy's mother, standing behind her son, her face hard, unreadable.

Jackson picks up his cup of chai. Amelia, remember that woman in Jaipur, the one with the arm missing below the elbow? He takes a sip of tea, looks at Reema who is crossing the road towards him, and raises his cup like a toast, because they are here together. He and Amelia had referred to the woman in Jaipur as the half-armed woman in every argument about her that followed. In 1968 they had taken two weeks' holiday to tour the north. Amelia had forbidden him to ask the woman the nature of the accident that had severed her forearm, had been angry with him for wanting to pry, but he had wanted to know what kind of woman she was. What kind of woman would offer to find them a child here in India, offer to make their lives complete, to give them a family?

'Thank you,' he says to the boy, in a way he never said thank you to the half-armed woman. He had never believed it was a kindness the woman was offering. She had told them she knew how to help them, that she had earmarked some children who might want to go home to Delhi with them, then back to America where the child would be safe and wealthy. Jackson had distrusted that a stranger could honestly consider the desires of a childless couple in their forties. Jackson and Amelia argued that night, Jackson defending the honour of his rich seed, Amelia shaking her head, her eyes looking through him to all the things that really mattered.

'You look better,' Reema says, as she arrives at the table, but she's not being truthful. He looks worse. Sometimes things get far worse before they get better, and this is something else she has learned from teaching young children. 'Much better.'

Jackson touches the bandage again. The pills he was given by the doctor are having some kind of effect, but it's a woozy one. He sits up straighter on his stool.

'The doctor — wasn't he much too young to be a doctor?' he says. She smiles, thinking that Pune is her only option. A bus pulls into the roadside chai stand and stirs wreaths of dust. Jackson closes his eyes and holds his breath, releases it with a cough. He covers his cup.

When he opens his eyes there are more people milling about the chai stand. The turbaned man and his horses are much farther up the road. He closes them again.

'I have more of the painkillers in my backpack. Anytime you need one, just tell me,' Reema says. He opens his eyes and looks up to see Yosh standing next to her.

'Hello,' Jackson says, as though they've been separated for a long time. He hears this strangeness in his own voice. Yosh squats down beside him.

'I'm sure we could have found another doctor who would say that stitches were necessary,' Yosh says. The roadside dust seems to settle. 'And that you probably shouldn't carry on with your trip.'

Jackson doesn't like to be difficult, not the cranky old man who has people walking on eggshells — like his father, who bellowed when he had a touch of flu. 'I'm tip-top,' he says.

Yosh stands again and looks around, and Reema thinks he might be searching for something more convincing to say.

'Do you know this town?' she asks him. He crouches again, squatting in perfect balance beside her.

'I have a friend who grew up in Gaggal. It was a small village, but now it has an airport. Or at least a D.L.H. runway.'

'D.L.H.?'

'Don't. Land. Here.'

His smile moves her. She looks up the road at Monica, who is still taking photographs.

'You might prefer the tea plantation in Palampur,' Yosh says, looking to Reema for confirmation. She nods. He turns to Jackson, 'Reema's family will take care of you, I'm sure.'

Reema dips her eyes. *Re, re, re* sings the bull.

Jackson shakes his head. Old men get questioned about whether they are sure of what they say, what they want, and this he finds tiring.

'He would like to go to the snow line,' Reema says. She will have to accompany him.

Yosh pulls over a stool from a nearby table and sits in front of one of the four steel cups.

'I would be very grateful,' Jackson says. The chai boy brings them more tea.

Amelia had asked the one-armed woman where the child she was offering them would come from. Which mother had wanted to give up a child and how could she possibly feel right about this? 'You are too thinking about these things,' the woman had said. 'You must trust that there is a child who needs you.' But Jackson had nixed the idea. Instead, he had thrown himself into his work on the Jayakwadi irrigation project in Maharashtra and had, each night, made a point of mounting his beautiful wife, determined and confident in his fertility and hers, which had been proven once if only briefly.

'It's not easy to know where the snow starts at this time of year,' Yosh says, nervously tapping the steel cup on the table. 'The snow line has been receding.' He taps a little louder.

Reema searches again for Monica. Who can she tell about why she must get some time on her own? She spots her photographing something at a stall that sells nuts and sundries. The sign above the fabric shop is for Surya Resorts in McLeodganj, Dharamsala, and boasts of luxury rooms and a well-stocked bar. Its slogan — *Your Home in the Hills* — is smeared with blue paint, making *Home* more like *om*. She watches to see if Monica will notice. Oh, little monkeys.

'Why does it have to be the snow?' Yosh asks Jackson.

'Because Amelia liked the snow,' Reema answers on his behalf. She understands why this is important to him. As they sat on the ground at Masroor, waiting for the police and the doctor, they talked softly to each other as she watched the scarf swell with blood from his wound. He is a man of strong feeling.

'We could go back to Pong Dam. They have more comforts there and we could see a better doctor,' Yosh says. But Jackson waves this off. He didn't come all the way here to quit now. The snow is the right solution. There was snow in Boston when she left him, slanted like the surface of a desert dune on their bedroom window sill. Amelia did not want to leave among roses and moths, flowers and hissing summer lawns. Amelia needed to feel the cold in order to leave.

'I'll get another car to take me,' Jackson says. Reema does a double take and catches Yosh's eye, which accuses her. *Is this what you wanted?*

'Jackson,' she says.

'What do you think is wrong with me?' Jackson asks them. He doesn't want to seem like a fool around these young people.

'I don't think anything is wrong with you,' Yosh says.

'Then you'll take me?'

Reema takes note of Yosh's knee beside Jackson's, the smoothly muscled one next to the diminished boniness of the other.

'I will make it worth your while,' Jackson says, thinking about how he used to be the life of the party, the joker — the one who would always say, really, do you have to take everything so seriously? Now look at him, intimidating young people like a curmudgeon.

'I don't care about the money,' Yosh says.

Reema looks at him to see if this is true. 'You won't find a reliable driver, just like that,' Reema says, and oh, little horse, come get her. That moment in the garden at the wedding when Jackson told her what he'd written on his tag and hung on the wishing tree — *Stay awake to each other* — perhaps that's what has fastened her to him. 'Not everyone is to be trusted, the way Yosh is,' she adds.

Jackson's face is like a child's when he turns to her and she knows she has no way out of this.

'I'll go with him,' she says to Yosh. 'I can see my family afterwards.' She recalculates her days and scrunches up the Pune brochure in her pocket. *Stay awake.* Jackson has words for love.

Vehicles honk in the road as Monica crosses to them.

Yosh is responsible for them all, translating, negotiating — and yet it's really Monica's agenda they should be following.

'It's not a huge diversion for us, I suppose,' Yosh says.

Jackson raises his arm as though someone has scored a goal —

117

perhaps a little over the top — as he smiles and nods a thank you to both of them. He looks around for the boy, to pay him, and sees him sitting in the shade. His mother has taken over and is clearing cups, rinsing them with small drops of water from a bucket, wiping them with her sari before she places them back on the tables. Her movements are precise, measured for efficiency and endurance. She takes a roll of rupee notes out of her blouse, unfolds them and counts quickly, seems satisfied with the total, and folds the fat roll of bills back together into her blouse. She brings sticks for the fire beneath her boiling water, spoons tea into small steel pots.

'What's the plan?' Monica says as she joins them.

'Still heading north,' Yosh says.

Jackson watches the chai boy stack cubes of brown sugar with his one hand, building a proud castle with the finest of materials. He wants to cry and doesn't understand why. He looks at Reema, then Yosh, then Monica. He looks back at the mother of the one-handed boy. The thing he needs to remember about Amritsar will make all the difference and will explain this nagging feeling that it is all his fault that Amelia is gone.

Monica takes up the cup that has been left for her. Jackson watches the fast fingers of the mother's hands as she lines up chai pots in a neat row, wipes each pot with her sari, and inside him something creaks like the hull of a wooden boat against a dock.

THIRTEEN

'When you cross the border into Tibet, the day lightens,' Monica says.

Reema looks over her shoulder and smiles at Monica in the back seat, a travel book open on her lap. She has been delivering commentary about the Himalayas regularly and with cheer throughout the journey from Masroor. Monica points out the Tibetan prayer flags strung between poles that line the road as the jeep climbs towards the town of McLeodganj. Reema looks up towards the sky in the spaces between buildings, to the red, blue, and yellow fluttering of the silk. This is not Tibet, but, yes, something is different here. The things Monica knows about India from books are bald and plain, but new to Reema, who is grateful for the points of interest, the arcane facts behind objects. Namgyal Monastery, Bhagsunath Temple, Church of St John's in the Wilderness. A career in finance is made by being on top of things, and Monica is a model of efficiency. Reema is not on top of anything, but now the time has come.

In search of conversation they have spoken about birthdays. Monica will be thirty-one years old in August. The numbers make Reema nervous; life can change in a second. Thirty-one is unimaginable and yet merely five years away. Yosh told them how he spent his early twenties in this area, learning yoga, going against everything in his background, after he ran away from his father's shoe business. Each time he returns to Dharamkot he feels he is coming home.

She looks at Yosh's hands on the steering wheel, the veins that run from his wrists to his knuckles protruding as the jeep hugs a corner. Hands he stands on, hands he holds in front of his chest in prayer position. The road ahead becomes dense with hotels, shops selling Tibetan hats, prayer bowls, teapots, the vendors in traditional dress, and farther up the road is a group of hippies in patterned clothes and blond dreadlocks.

Yosh tells them the town changes when the Dalai Lama returns to the temple from his missions abroad. Tibetans come out in great numbers, he says, lining the streets to greet the vehicle that brings him safely home; they wave and throw flowers. Reema had arrived in Pathankot to a similar fanfare as she disembarked from the overnight train from Delhi. The politician who had been in a private carriage was greeted by a crowd gathered with bouquets of flowers, with more along the road that led towards the town. Jyoti's friend told her that the crowd for the Health Minister was normal for politicians. Forget your rock stars and film stars, he said. Here, government officials keep these people sweet on them, and in return get the crowds and garlands of marigolds.

'Look,' Monica says, and Reema turns to follow her finger towards the road sign along the steep curve: *We like you but we don't like your speed*. There is something to be said about a transport minister with a sense of humour.

They arrive at the Dalai Lama's temple, and Monica gets out of the car to take photos. Reema looks over her shoulder to Jackson in the back seat. He is asleep, his mouth open, a touch of saliva in the corner of his lips.

———

I have responsibilities, I yell from the door and the Bombay apartment echoes while Mr A. A. A. Siddiqui waits for me at Jayakwadi to check the Japanese generator, and you yell back 'What about your responsibilities to me,' with the telephone number of the one-armed woman in your hand, the taxi idling in the street below.

———

The Pink House Hotel and Spa on Jogiwara Road is like a doll's house that Reema once owned. She had started by arranging the miniature furniture she'd received as presents at the age of seven and collected small additions as the months wore on. For her eighth birthday, her parents bought her a four-storey structure with moveable walls that could make rooms bigger or smaller as she wished. By age nine she had stopped being interested in interiors and tiny beds, tiny chairs, tiny washstands, or the tiny blond dolls that came from Hamleys; instead she enjoyed the house's architecture. She liked to take down walls, expand or contract rooms and build extensions. She created terraces with lookout points, so that each of the four storeys had a different angle on the landscape. Every occupant of the house would live equally well, with a view, she insisted, and this commune-like life would be full of music.

This terrace at the back of the Pink House Hotel looks

out towards mountains on the other side of the valley, one slope green with a terraced garden of its own. The lime green umbrellas sheltering the tables make for crude symmetry. Reema sits beside Monica, who takes out her notebook and turns the page to another list. She crosses off one of the items and Reema wonders what it is that they have accomplished by sitting here. Next Monica lifts her camera and photographs the surroundings. Snow peaks, rocky crags, terraced valley farms. Jagged structures built into slopes. Check. Perhaps Monica was also a girl who got tired of the interiors of her doll's houses.

A backpacker in a striped handwoven vest comes into Reema's view. They lock gazes and for a moment her heart races. She has little experience of men like him and wonders what he sees in her. She turns away. It's not her interest in him that makes her heart race; it's her interest in his life. She wants to be like him, to make friends with strangers from all over the world, all of her belongings in a single pack on her back.

'TripAdvisor was right,' Monica says, as she puts the lens cover back on her camera. 'Beautiful place.' She places the camera on the table next to Yosh, who is deep in concentration over a map.

It's chilly. Reema adjusts her pashmina around her shoulders. She shouldn't have drawn Yosh and Monica further into this by telling them about what's in Jackson's suitcase.

Jackson farts. He looks up from his jasmine tea at her, sheepish. 'Once a man, twice a child,' he says. They both giggle. This is now a routine between them. During their meal last night, she asked him how the prawns in his momos were. 'Fine,' he said, 'a little old. I can relate.'

'Look,' she says, and points. The snow in the distance is not that high up.

'I told you Yosh could pull strings with the man upstairs,' Jackson says. Reema smiles, catching Yosh's eye. She worries that she might have winked. She looks at the side of the building next door, which features a billboard-sized cotton poster that flaps in the breeze: *Tibet: One People, One Nation. Fifty years of Resistance 1959–2009.* She keeps her eyes there for as long as she can.

Yosh is not a flirter. He is not the kind of man to make a move; he is the kind of man who knows that moves are irrelevant, who likes her because she knows this too.

'I remember my mother telling me about the Dalai Lama when I was a little boy,' Yosh says. 'She made him out to be already an old man, who would just die off or be killed like Gandhi.'

'You had interesting conversations in your house,' Reema says, referring to their talk on the drive up. She doesn't look at him. His tyrant father who still threatens to cut off any support unless Yosh returns to the shoe factory is in stark contrast to this mother who talks of the Dalai Lama. When Jackson mentioned Yosh's Hinduism, Yosh cut him off, correcting: 'No, not a Hindu,' shutting Jackson down.

She turns to Monica, who stares out at the view. Reema checks her watch to gauge the time in London, to imagine where Robert is now, asleep or waking, making breakfast, on his way to work in his tight jacket. They have planned another Skype call but thanks to time zones they will both be sleepy. Perhaps that is the way they should stay, not awake to each other the way the wishing-tree tag asks, but instead sleepy and distant and easy. Every morning she feels nauseous, and so every morning she hates him and Rudyard Kipling. When she is sleepy she is kinder.

Jackson surveys the young people around him. He doesn't remember being young, but he's sure he was never so serious.

'Someone once asked Gandhi what he thought of western civilisation,' he says, sitting forward in his plastic chair, holding his finger up like a prophet, 'and you know what he said?' The others wait, but he senses they know this one. He wags the finger: 'He said "I think that would be a very good idea."' Monica laughs, the other two smile and, well, a man has to try.

Across the valley, the buildings on the terraced slopes look lopsided and unstable. There are animal shapes in the drifting clouds, and as Jackson spots one that looks like a whale, Yosh calls out to the hotel manager, who has stepped out onto the terrace. He waves him over to the table, and Jackson stands to greet him. Reema marvels at how swift and strong he is when it comes to this old-fashioned formality. The others remain seated.

'Beautiful spot,' Jackson says as he shakes the man's hand. He sits down again.

'I wish you a happy stay,' the man says. Jackson had taken an instant liking to this Kashmiri man when they'd arrived at the reception desk last night.

'There was trouble in these parts last year, was there not?' Jackson had asked him as they waited for help with their luggage.

'In Tibet, not here.'

'But it affected the community here, yes?'

'Yes,' the man said, hesitantly.

'Shooting?'

'None here, but in Tibet, after the Chinese government cracked down on protesters.'

'Oh yes?'

'They shot thirty Tibetans in Sichuan — smashed in their faces,' the manager had said, letting down his guard, bitterness on his face, his allegiance with the Tibetans obvious.

Now Jackson points to the billboard, and as he and the owner discuss this anniversary of the first Tibet uprising, Reema watches her companions, trying not to focus on Yosh alone.

There will be protests, there have already been killings and abductions in Tibet, and the owner is worried that the Chinese will mark the anniversary with violence here in Dharamsala. Reema feels the hair on her arms rise at the sound of the tools of resistance. A whisper, a letter, a horse, some bread, one shoulder touching another and another, standing in a row.

'One day Tibet will be free again, but Dharamsala will never be a normal Indian town,' the manager says. 'But don't worry,' he adds quickly, as though remembering that frightened tourists are bad for business. He bows his head before wishing them a good day and heading back inside.

Reema tries to gauge what Yosh is thinking as he stares at the terrace floor. Just as time stops, just as old men can read minds, some people can intuit the future. Yoga shows you what is next, in your body, in life. You start fast; you end up lying down.

'Oh no!' Monica says.

Reema turns to see her reaching for the knapsack beside her. She takes out a slim, neatly organised first aid kit, unzips it and pulls out cotton balls.

'It's bleeding again,' Monica says, as she touches Jackson's forehead. She wipes the blood that has begun to trickle towards his eye.

Reema lifts up the edge of the plaster and peeks beneath it, but she has no idea what to look for or what to do if she finds it.

'My medication,' Jackson says, and he waves his hand in the air, shooing away the annoying daily warfarin tablet that is responsible for his stomach pain and dizziness, and the thinness of his blood. Damn it, can he not just get a break to get this done?

'We should get to a doctor,' Yosh says.

Jackson shakes his head. 'No, definitely not.' With the mountain air and the peaks in sight, he feels confident his task will be completed. The mountains give him new courage. When he returns to Boston, spring will have arrived in his neighbourhood and shoots of malachite green leaves will be on the trees; robins will be perched on his backyard fence. Perhaps his delay is all about that: he is delaying the moment of standing with the tea canister dumped out into a lake, a river, a snow bank, into anything — because spring alone without her in Boston will be unbearable. He senses the arrhythmia of his heart and again he is in Amritsar at the small stall with the rows of pinnis, balushahis and gur ka halwa, the cauldrons of frying samosas. The rickshaw passes again, and he is squeezed out of the road into an alley near the Golden Temple.

'Yosh knows a doctor here,' Reema says, squeezing his hand.

He looks into her face. She said at the wedding that young people are lost and think only of themselves, but this is not true. He takes her hand in his and smiles at her.

'Amelia and I did a trek in these mountains when we were young. There was snow,' he says.

'I have checked this, and the snow is very high up this year ...' Yosh says. He tells them that the top of Triund will not produce the results he's looking for.

'It was the same time of year, I'm sure of it,' Jackson says.

'But higher up ...'

When he and Amelia hiked in this area, there were people to help them, guide them — not professionals, just ordinary people who said they'd show them the way. Come here, look at this, a young boy said as he took them to a waterfall at the back of the pass. People were so kind. And Amelia, do you remember, the bones we found in the pass and what the boy said: that they were the bones of a langur monkey and that he had seen the langurs visit the bones and mourn and wail like humans over one of their dead. The boy said that there were some who saw the bones dance, saw them move off dancing into the forest, because they had been properly mourned. Amelia, even the bones danced.

'I can find some help to take me up, I think,' Jackson says.

Reema and Yosh exchange looks. Monica dips her eyes to her first aid kit.

'Let me see what the manager thinks,' Yosh says.

Jackson releases Reema's hand, wipes his mouth with his fingers, looks to the sky, and, oh, there in the mountains, is a cap of white close enough for him to touch, shimmering like an Alberta winter.

My brother grabs the boy by the coat and tosses him into the snow bank. Tired of the teasing, tired of losing, my brother picks up a stone. The other bully runs off. I step back. My brother is bigger. He has weapons. He has become a man.

FOURTEEN

'Every Accident is an Act of Neglect,' Monica says from the back seat, reading aloud another road sign as the jeep turns sharply left. She doesn't seem to enjoy the humour in these transport ministry warnings the way Reema does. A cow rests in the road ahead. A car approaches, coming down the hill, and both the jeep and the car go around the cow. Reema feels the wheel below her slip off the road into the dirt, then back onto the road again. Perhaps this far beyond the Dalai Lama's temple, the road surface itself gets less attention. 'Safety is not Expensive, it's Priceless,' says a sign a little farther down.

Yosh turns the jeep off onto a small dirt track. They climb and twist, higher and higher.

———

The jeep can go no farther; they have reached the end of the road and now there is only a path of grass with rocks like moles pocking skin. They have bumped their way to the Gallu Devi Temple; the trees have become shorter, the evergreens darker. To their left is a sign that introduces the Rest Awhile Café. Jackson sees that the path beyond it is only for walking humans or beasts of burden. Yosh gets out of the jeep and surveys the area. Jackson follows and stands beside him, and they both look up towards the peaks. The snow is many hours' walk above them, and not on Triund, but on a different mountain summit altogether.

'I hope you understand now,' Yosh says. He takes a deep breath and exhales slowly. Jackson feels ashamed.

He wants to apologise, but nothing comes out. Yosh is a fine man. A man who holds himself in, the way a jar holds water. Jackson walks back towards the café, one foot in front of the other, hoping for a solution. Toes. Heels. Toes.

Amelia, how not to fail you? He stops then sits on a large tree stump at the side of the road.

'You pride yourself on your bad humour,' Amelia had said, disappointment in her eyes. They had known each other for eight days, each of them on holiday with their parents in Brunei. He had kissed her in the Sultan's tropical garden at midnight on Christmas Eve; she had kissed him back. The New Year in Brunei meant that his father had two more years on his contract while Britain reopened the oil wells that they had filled with concrete to foil the Japanese during the war. Oil was gushing; Jackson's father's career was on a high. When the Sultan's friend whispered over gin and tonic that the Sultan had ascended to the throne at eleven years old and had an erection for the first ten years of his reign, Jackson had laughed but his dutiful father frowned. Jackson was young, everything was as it should be, and there was Amelia, surrounded by other guests at the Christmas party, singing as her mother played the piano ... *There's a tree in the meadow, with a stream drifting by, and carved upon that tree I see 'I love you till I die'*... her voice kinder than Margaret Whiting's version, her cheeks quivering, her eyes closed.

It's no wonder he proposed the next day. But Amelia thought it was a joke. She did not trust him because he teased and poked fun at everything. If something had weight, he undercut it with a laugh because the feeling was too much.

He was returning to his new job on the Bhakra Dam project in Punjab, and she with her parents back to the States, to her final year of teacher's college at Columbia, and oh, 1950 was going to be torture. They spent the rest of the holiday holding hands, sneaking kisses, talking about how America was a promise they were both unsure of, and listening to music. Jackson was lost in her voice. In the evenings, perched beside the Sultan's grand piano, she sang in perfect inflections of Doris Day, of Dinah Shore, of many others. Who would not have to tell a joke?

The men in kurtas have fallen upon the woman in the headscarf. She has called out. My mind has heard, my hands are hearing, my lips are hearing, even my knees hear, but my feet are deaf. Wait. Don't. *But I don't move.*

Reema and Monica climb past where Jackson is sitting, and stop close to where Yosh stands staring out towards the trees. Monica puts her hands on her hips and follows his gaze.

'I guess it's a proper climb,' Reema says, seeing Monica's unhappiness.

'Not what I came to India for,' Monica says.

Two stray mutts scrounge for food on the steps that lead up to a different resting spot, the Sun and Moon café, with its Coca-Cola sign and the blue tarpaulin draped over the sticks that form its roof.

'I understand,' Reema says.

'I came to get away from old white guys who make all the decisions.'

The dogs snarl and bark and someone in the café shoos them off, but they continue their barking at something in the branches beyond the first line of trees.

'He's unreasonable,' Monica says, facing her.

Reema feels accused. 'He's an old man,' she says. It has an effect. The slippery, knowing moment they shared at Masroor returns, and Monica's eyes search Reema's face.

'Yeah, we will all be old …' she says.

The sound of drums and chanting comes from Gallu Temple a little below them. 'There was a story my auntie once told me about ghosts,' Monica continues. 'A ghost that walks with its feet turned backwards. She said that's how it feels to lose someone in your life — like you're walking with your feet turned backwards.' She nods in Jackson's direction.

The drumming and chanting from the temple grow louder. Reema watches as the mutts on the steps of the café wrap around each other in play, entangled like serpents around the rod of Hermes, a low growl from both.

'I'll see how he's doing,' Reema says.

When she reaches Jackson he has his small knapsack on his lap, has unzipped it and is looking inside. He looks up at her. 'We could make a sling and shoot me up like a pebble!' he says.

She sits down beside him on the boulder.

'I'm so sorry. I am wasting your time,' he says.

He waits for her to speak, expecting her to scold him, but her face does not look angry. It's less than a week since she was cross with him on the meadow at the reservoir. When Amelia was angry with him she would freeze him out. They rarely argued or confronted each other about their small bruises or selfish snubs. They recovered alone, missed the other, and came back unchanged. This worked for them. Things are so different for these young people, always talking things through, always clearing the air, always behaving like they are lying on Freud's couch. What a different man he would have to be now, if he were young.

'Why not try to walk a bit more? We could just have a look. And, you know, the snow will come. Maybe not until December, but it will come,' she says.

Does she believe the things she's saying? She could be in Pune singing ragas. By staying with Jackson in the north she has cemented her visit to her rich cousins in Palampur, whose gold-grade tea has won prizes in London and Amsterdam, and who in any case would never have forgiven her if she'd gone south.

She checks her phone. She has missed a call from Robert. A whisper, a letter, a horse, some bread, a shoulder, she thinks. If she screams here it will echo in the mountains.

'If you say so, then. Why not?' Jackson zips up the small daypack and slips it on. The tea canister shifts to the centre of his back and his eyes fall closed for a second; the dizziness is like a veil that brushes past his face. *There's a tree in the meadow.* He begins to walk up the path again.

The beginning of the trail is level. He feels strong. In the early days of his retirement Amelia would sing all through the house, all day. He would move from room to room, lost as to what to do with himself, and the sound of her voice would rise, and she would become one of her favourite singers — Brenda Lee, Patsy Cline, Etta James.

I fall to pieces, each time I see you again ... I fall to pieces ... how can I be just your friend.

At first he believed she was singing because she was happy, but with each song he heard something else: something lost to her that possibly he had taken away by being in her space all day long. Eventually he stopped tromping a path through his own kitchen, living room and study, and he stayed in the basement fixing his trains, doing puzzles, crosswords, reading his newspapers and books on India, and wishing he knew, after all these years, how not to annoy her. He would be grumpy with his toast that was burnt on the corner, with the sink that would clog for no reason at all, with the constant wind that would blow in March — grumpy mostly because he didn't understand why the unease between them was his fault.

He walks briskly, past Monica and Yosh, who stay put as they watch him go by, with Reema on his heels. She touches his shirt as he lurches ahead of her. How wrong he has been about so many things. He should have been braver. He walks faster. The world is on fire. Only snow will do. The edge of the tea canister in his daypack rubs against his spine. Don't you ever listen, Jackson? Don't you ever learn?

'Wait for me,' Reema says, and takes his hand. Hers is small. Warm. He will not let himself cry.

She squeezes his hand and they slow down. It's steeper than he thought. He stops, takes a deep breath, starts again, looking up towards a slope where, still, the snow refuses to appear.

'Jackson,' Reema says softly. She strokes his hand, the skin as soft as crepe. She wishes she had never spoken to him at the wedding. But here she is. 'You can't go charging off like that.'

There is a rustling in the forest to her right. She stops and searches for the source. High above them, a branch bends, leaves fall, another tree moves. She can't be sure, but she thinks she has seen a body the size of a young boy, silver fur covering the arms and torso, black face, a halo of white fur framing it. This one so different from those on the meadow. Come, monkey.

Jackson stops again, panting now. He's perspiring.

There's a large flat rock at the side of the path. 'Sit,' Reema says, 'This is foolish. We don't need to go further. Sit.'

He obeys, and she joins him. 'I think you're right,' he says. He hears a rushing in his ears, looks behind him for a waterfall, but there's only grass and more rock, and a scattering of Himalayan oak trees that have been lopped for firewood. The rushing begins to subside then flares again. He glances sideways at Reema to see if she's hearing it too, but her face is serious, her eyes searching back along the trail for Yosh and Monica. A sound in the trees behind them makes them both turn. Jackson catches sight of the white border around the black face of the monkey.

'Ah!' he says and points. 'Langur.'

'It's huge,' she says.

'They are special.'

'I've never seen such a big monkey.'

The langur leaps away.

'A man I met here many years ago told me that the langurs hiccup. A group of them will hiccup when they come across another group,' Jackson says. 'Isn't that something?'

Reema thinks carefully about this possibility. 'Maybe it only sounds like a hiccup, but hiccups are involuntary, so … maybe it's a surprise reaction.'

'He spent a long time up here. He eventually left when his favourite dog was killed by a leopard.' He pauses, looks at her serious face. 'I wonder if the dog was named Spot,' he says, but he can see that Reema is not amused.

He adjusts his knapsack, swings it forward on his lap, with the tea canister inside now perched on his knee. They sit in silence; the leaves rustle behind them. Birds sing.

'My brother's children have moved far away — one lives in Dubai and the other in Australia,' Jackson says. The leaves rustle again and there's a flurry of caws and twitters. 'He's not a happy man.' He sighs. He lowers the knapsack to the ground as if to put the tea canister out of range of what he is about to say.

'So many men in marriages as long as mine have affairs,' he says. Reema looks at him and he can see that this topic does not shock her. 'For years and years, some of them. Double lives, even, whole other families.' She nods, as though she knows of this, but she couldn't, he thinks; no one this young knows anything.

'But me?' He shakes his head, which settles the rushing in his ears. He continues to shake it and to smile, because he has always wanted to tell a young person this. Young people don't know how love is done. They strut and rut and yell and walk away. 'I only ever wanted Amelia's body. No one else was right.'

Reema smiles. 'You're very lucky,' she says. Reema's father believes he is a modern man, but he secretly despises the fact that his daughter has her own flat in London and can wander around Kilburn at night, meet men in bars, welcome them into her bed, between her sheets, between her legs. A courtesan of the Kama Sutra. He moved away from India for reasons that she has yet to fully grasp. Even the music began to disappoint him, as though his upbringing in California had inspired dreams that couldn't come true here. The articles he posts to her, from his home a few miles across London in East Finchley, are about danger, danger everywhere you look, Reema. He would die of shame if his daughter moved to India to stand in the streets with other women to protest sexual violence, to bare her shoulders and lie down in the road in solidarity. But for Reema it would be a chance to free the dark-skinned Indian woman buried deep within her.

Her mind feels foggy. 'Jackson,' she says, and could this be the moment?

'Yes?'

In Year Seven at Mill Hill School, Reema was given a badge for perseverance. She stood at the front of assembly to receive the honour from Miss Lang, who praised her work with the Year Ones and their nativity play at Christmas. Miss Lang read from a scroll that she later handed to Reema and which then hung on her dormitory wall for the remainder of her time at school. The words on the scroll were about tasks, about tenacity. *If that task be great or small, do it well or not at all.*

In all the years the scroll hung on the wall at Mill Hill, and through all the visits from her parents who came to pick her up on weekends, nothing was ever said about the words written there, about their appropriateness, their pressure, or indeed the prison the words built around Reema. She looks at the mole below Jackson's ear with its coarse white hair.

'I'm tired. Let's go back to the hotel,' she says. 'We'll find the right place for Amelia.'

FIFTEEN

'Now fall forward. Without effort. Don't force the fold.'

Standing in front of her, Yosh makes this falling forward sound easy. But Reema feels light-headed, so she doesn't fold at all, but runs her hands down her thighs and holds on to her knees. She turns her head to the right to see that Monica is touching the floor, her stance as sure as a tree trunk. The three of them fill Yosh's room. The Pink House Hotel interior is humble in its Tibetan decor, and the wood floor has just space enough for their three mats. Jackson is still asleep down the hall, and the sun has not yet made an appearance from behind the mountain that wheezes out a kind of judgement of her inflexibility.

When she asked Yosh if she could join them for yoga this morning, he hesitated. 'Don't feel you have to,' he said eventually, but there was more. 'You don't need to try so hard.'

'What?'

'I know I do it too, but why do you indulge him?'

She had seen the way that Yosh was polite, generous and yet wary of Jackson.

'I'm the one who asked him along,' she said.

Yosh held up his palm to her in a gesture that said he didn't disagree.

Now as he guides them through the practice, she is challenged by what he didn't say.

'And look up. Your back is flat here … now walk back to become a plank.'

She does as he says, counts as she balances on both hands, her feet supporting her legs, her body parallel to the floor. Her arms wobble. Beside her Monica's breathing sounds like ocean waves, and Reema imitates it, focusing on the back of her throat. Yoga is a space where you are not supposed to think, only to breathe.

Last night during dinner at the Tibetan café with Monica and Jackson, Yosh asked her what she knew about yoga.

'It's difficult,' she said. *Find peace where there is no peace.*

In describing to the group how he had left New York and his father's now international business, his voice cracked, as though the same thing making his father rich was making him ill. He had tried to be the dutiful son. He became more steeled when he described the irony of having to move to America to discover Buddhism and Ambedkar, the champion of Dalits who damned Hinduism.

'I ran away from here, and on the Pacific Coast I'm outside all of it,' he said.

No caste, no culture, no religion. She let her fingers brush the napkin on the table between them.

After dinner, as they walked ahead of Monica and Jackson towards the hotel, he told her that as a child his father had not been allowed to drink from the same well as higher-caste villagers, or to worship in the same temple, but he had vowed to himself that one day he would be a big man. Yosh's father studied hard, made it through high school. When he married Yosh's mother, he was moving up. Her family owned a small shoe workshop. He taught himself English, Tamil, Punjabi, Russian, German, and then 'magic took place in India,' Yosh said, turning to her with a sarcastic grin. Economic reforms and foreign investment in the country meant that his father's small factory could begin to sell shoes to the world.

'My father returned to his village in a BMW and paid for the repair of the temple. The villagers were forced to accept his generosity,' he said. 'My father is a rich bastard.'

Reema laughed but quickly realised Yosh wasn't joking. He rubbed his left wrist. 'I don't want his money.'

'Does it hurt?' she asked, looking at his wrist.

'An old injury from when I first started yoga.' He told her about the master he had met in Dharamkot, how he had tried so hard to please him, wanted so hard not to be beaten, the way he had been by his own father, that he tried a pose before he was ready, had fallen and broken his wrist.

Now, she drops her belly to the floor, pushes up on her hands, arches her spine and throws her head back to look at the ceiling. His voice moves her into a position that he does not call downward dog, as they do in London. Each pose has its proper name. Yosh's life has been shaped by the place his body occupies in the world. From poor man to rich. Breathe. From teenager to man. Breathe. From Delhi to Vancouver. Breathe. Outside all of it. Breathe. Like this it is possible to go from one thing to the next. She walks up to her hands, gets to her feet, bends back and then brings her hands together to stand and rest. 'Tadasana,' he says, and she exhales.

As they continue the practice she goes in and out of focus on the movements. She watches Monica, whose body is supple, her legs yielding, her arms easily bent in prayer position behind her back.

Reema thinks that Canada must be full of space to breathe. Yosh said he lives in a neighbourhood where there are many Indians, Hispanics, Vietnamese, Chinese, and Indigenous people. Though he has made friends in many communities, he avoids Indians, he said, because they are the ones who ask him about his name, know his caste, don't trust him to teach yoga. Meanwhile the rents in his neighbourhood are rising, and if he does not secure a steady income from a West End yoga studio soon, he will have to move. Breathe. Further east is further away from the ocean, and this he doesn't want.

She keeps her spine straight and twists over her right knee as instructed. This feels good. She looks over her other shoulder. Monica's outstretched fingertips nearly touch hers, her arms confident in the pose.

When daylight nudges the dark mountain, Reema is in the corpse pose. *Nothing to do, nothing to be …*

Her only gaze is internal, like watching the scree and scrub that line the slope of a mountain inside her. A faint bell rings and she's brought back to the room.

'Just take your time. Stretch your arms and legs as you need to. When you're ready, roll over on your right side,' Yosh says.

She turns onto her side, with no desire to sit up.

'Push yourself up,' Yosh says.

As she does so, she opens her eyes and the counting starts again, the calculation of days. Yosh's eyes are still closed. She stares at his top lip, the Cupid's bow. She looks over at Monica, seated, eyes also closed. Nothing moves in the room.

Yosh does not ask them to do an 'om' together as they do in London classes. She has never felt comfortable with this shared humming among strangers.

'How was it?' he asks, when he finally opens his eyes.

'Great,' Monica says.

He looks at Reema. 'Yes,' she says. 'I'm not good at meditation.'

He nods.

She lowers her eyes. Come, little fish.

'Do you have something you'd like to do today?' Yosh asks Monica.

'What would you suggest?'

Reema adjusts the straps of her camisole, takes hold of the band that holds her hair in a ponytail and pulls it off, allowing her hair to fall over her eyes.

'Norbulingka, perhaps,' he says, 'the Tibetan crafts institute.'

'Yes, okay.'

'They have beautiful things,' he says.

'I'll stay with Jackson,' Reema says. 'We'll figure out what he needs to do.'

Yosh releases his lotus position.

There's silence again.

'He really should go back to Pong Dam. It's more comfortable for him there,' Monica says.

They are both right: Jackson should not be here, should not be dictating what is going on for any of them. She's an idiot.

'I was a boy in Chandrapur when my father met an American man who Jackson reminds me of. He had a lot of charm,' Yosh says, shrugs, and smiles.

Reema thinks of the man near the Old Delhi train station, on a bench, asleep with his hands between his knees, three children curled together beneath the bench, their feet sticking out onto the pavement, their faces black with dirt, clothes torn. The small boys collecting plastic cups to wash and sell. The cigarette vendors. The houses of sticks and tarpaulin. She traces a line of light that is beginning to angle sharply through the window, between the bed and the spot where Yosh sits on the wooden floor, his knees still in shadow.

'And did you like the man?' she asks.

He takes a moment to consider this. Reema wonders about Chandrapur, what a child there does. Had Yosh, as a little boy, turned discarded steel and meshing into toys — for beating, for steering, for weapons — the kinds of toys she saw her brother play with?

'I did,' he says.

Reema uncrosses her legs and stretches them out in front of her, massaging her knees. Yosh's childhood is nothing she can conjure except via her father's clippings. Dalits raped, burned and sliced, all over India. One boy, who had been wearing a watch that his attacker couldn't believe had belonged to him, had his hand cut off above the wrist.

'I'm starving,' Monica says.

A yoga teacher in London once told Reema's class that yoga performs internal cleansing: thick blood is dirty and causes disease in the body. The heat from the vinyasa cleans the blood and makes it thin, circulating freely, taking away pain, removing impurities. She wonders what is true. Breathe.

She draws her knees up to her chest and hugs them.

They sit in silence. The sharp sun has now reached Yosh's thigh.

Sixteen

Jackson, you are slow, you are dithering. You must get the job done. The morning sunlight has peeked over the mountain and lights up the corridor of the hotel's second floor. He lifts each foot in its canvas shoe up high as he walks from his room towards the yoga teacher's. It's circulation he needs, simply — all he needs is a walk, some fresh air and clear thoughts. And to talk to Yosh.

He raises his foot again, high, and sees Reema and the Canadian girl coming out of the yoga teacher's room. He stops. Ah, Amelia … things were not like this in our day. He waits until they turn the corner, headed for their respective rooms, before he continues. Amelia, young people are always interesting.

Perhaps there is a temple, here in McLeodganj, where he would be allowed to leave his wife. The mountains would protect her, there would eventually be snow, and the Tibetans are gentle.

He knocks on Yosh's door.

'Good morning, good morning, hope I'm not disturbing,' he says when he sees the face of the yoga teacher, who might have been hoping for someone else.

'Morning. How are you today?'

'A little slow, but not too bad, thank you.' Jackson adjusts his stance on the floor to keep himself tall. 'I was wondering if you were going out, and, if you are, whether I could join you for the walk.' He doesn't want to ask in advance about seeing a temple. 'I would like to exchange some money.'

Yosh doesn't answer immediately, and Jackson worries. He doesn't want to be burden. 'Never mind,' he says. 'I'm sorry — presumptuous of me.'

'I need to exchange some too, so yes, you can come with me,' Yosh says.

'Excellent.'

When Yosh asks him to give him a minute to get ready, Jackson waits outside the door.

———

They walk the winding road through McLeodganj. The morning air is crisp. Jackson walks as quickly as he can, not wanting to hold Yosh back. Market stalls come alive, one after the other: a woman takes chimes and cups from their newspaper cocoons; a man pours jewellery from a hessian sac and paws it onto the silk covering the table. Jackson sees in their faces that they are Tibetan; others, from what he knows of their dress, are Kashmiri.

'When I was in the Punjab as a young man, there was war in Kashmir,' Jackson says.

Yosh looks around them as if to see what has made Jackson mention such a thing.

'I know it's still a problem,' Jackson adds, defensively.

The vendors arrange teapots, singing bowls, beads, pashminas, and numerous small trinkets, like a collection of all the things that have been lost over a lifetime. Jackson touches the sleeve of Yosh's

Gore-Tex windbreaker and gives him a look of apology for slowing them down. They stop in front of a stall of woollen caps and thick yak-hair sweaters.

'Last year I had to cancel a tour for Americans in Jammu, Kashmir. They thought it was too unsafe. And more Kashmiris have come to live in Himachal Pradesh.'

'I was once a young man who could climb in the Pir Panjal,' Jackson says, and is proud he has remembered the name.

Yosh nods. 'We should move on?' He tucks his chin deep into the collar of his jacket.

Jackson keeps up with Yosh, certain that the yogi is walking more slowly for his sake, but with the incline in the road he is unable to go faster. Yosh is a gentle man, Jackson thinks, but also a man with a fan of scars on his back that have not been accounted for. There are events in this country that hit headlines around the world — the Gujarat riots, the Mumbai bombing last year — and Yosh has likely seen more than Jackson has imagined.

'Why did you leave after your training? It's so beautiful here,' Jackson says.

Yosh shrugs, yet searches to be polite. 'I returned to Delhi to help my mother.'

They come to a shop with electronics and phones. Yosh tells him he'll be just a moment, enters, leaving Jackson in front of the shop wondering about the young man's leanings. What help did his mother need? A few years ago, the Lashkar-e-Taiba, Islamist fundamentalists, declared jihad against India. Two days before Diwali they exploded bombs in two Delhi markets. These are reasons enough for a young man to move to the Pacific Coast of Canada.

The young village girl who comes to clean and wash the clothes, and make the beds, has her head bowed and Amelia is scowling. 'How dare you?' Amelia says and smells the nape of the girl's neck. This is nothing, I think, and I walk outside to the garden where there is the smell of champa flowers and cow dung.

Yosh emerges from the shop and they walk. At the far end of the market near a café adjacent to the temple of the Dalai Lama, a small crowd is gathering. The men and some women are shaven-headed and wearing saffron robes, fold upon fold of material that falls around their arms. Some carry placards, one of which says, 'DALAI LAMA STOP LYING'.

'What is happening?' Jackson says.

Yosh listens carefully to the conversations and chanting.

'I don't know. They are a rival faction of Buddhists. Maybe it has to do with what the hotel manager was talking about.'

Jackson looks carefully at their clean robes — they are not made of shreds of discarded cloth, rat-chewed and bloodstained, like traditional monks' robes. These look spun by machines.

Parked near the growing crowd is a white minivan, engine running, back door open, with boxes of trinkets spilling out. A Tibetan man, in simple cotton Toethung, and another Tibetan man, in western clothing, are shouting at each other. They stand beside the van and point to the boxes of Buddha heads, miniature prayer wheels, scrolls, and rolls of curry-coloured silk that spool out onto the road.

The protestors begin chanting as the men continue to shout. Yosh looks behind him. Jackson follows his gaze to see an opposing group of protesters coming from the temple. Suddenly there is a crash and someone yells. Jackson turns to see the Tibetan man in traditional dress splayed out over his boxes. The other man shouts and walks off towards the chanting protestors, in front of whom he spits.

Yosh takes Jackson by the arm. 'Let's go,' he says.

———

A driver, known to the Sultan of Brunei himself, has dropped us off at a beach, where we walk hand in hand. As we throw off our shoes, I pretend not to look at your legs. We kiss near the base of a palm tree. I touch your skin, lick your shoulder. On our way back to the car you drop my hand suddenly, looking down, standing still: a patterned scarf, a delicate beaded shoe, both spotted with blood. You will not hold my hand the entire next day.

SEVENTEEN

The sheets are cold. Jackson watches his index finger, with the swollen knobs that twist it like a witch's, as it refuses to lie flat on the bed. He has been sitting for many minutes, or even hours, since returning to the hotel with Yosh. He can't be sure how long. He does not move anything except his eyes from his finger to his big toe. The nail is like budding yeast. His breath is shallow. Are you there? He will not panic. This shallowness has happened once before. He waits. Are you there? He swallows. He places both hands on the bed beside him and wonders if he can push himself up. But everything is faster and more and more shallow, and he can only observe it. He waits.

The Sinclair Oil Refinery vet has his foot on the head of the struggling mare. He lassoes the front hooves; the farmer has secured the back two. Hold tight, oh fuck, it's butt first … push it back. I look around in a panic, through the dust, for Dad, because the word breech *is a syllable of pain. The farmer heels the foal back into the uterus, pushing up, up, to turn it around.* Ino empujen! *The farmer releases his rope. I stand back from the spray of shit and blood. 'We're going to have to get a third man to stitch up that anus,' the vet says when the foal is sprung free.*

Eighteen

She hums. This happens when she is angry with herself. A melody comes from holding the anger in. She doesn't want Yosh to hear it, so she walks quickly ahead of him towards the medical clinic. The wind has picked up and there are clouds over the peaks of the mountains.

'His office won't be open for another ten minutes,' Yosh calls after her.

She slows down, swallows the sounds, decisions, miscalculations — why didn't she consider that an old man could feel ill at this altitude?

'Do you sing professionally?' Yosh says.

She stops and looks at him. His face is kind; he's not teasing her the way Robert might. They start walking again, more slowly.

'No,' she says. Robert wants her to sing pop songs, get a record deal. Worse singers get them all time, he says. 'Do you sing at all? You didn't join my choir.'

'My family is very practical,' Yosh says finally. 'No one sings.'

'But you like music?'

A short pause before he says, 'God's there.'

He says it the way he might have said *that car is red*. The mere fact of god as simple as pointing out the colour of an object and finding it true. No. She speeds up again, does not like it when people speak this way; it's too bald. She likes a sentence to have edges, corners.

A gust of wind blows her hair across her eyes. She adjusts her posture to match his. His shoulders are straight, and his back sits on his hips as though aligned with hinges. *God's there. The car is red.* His neck. His arms. His skin.

Jackson's hand was cold, his forehead damp as she sat on the edge of his bed in his room asking, over and over, what was wrong, while he shook his head to indicate nothing was wrong. Clearly there was something wrong.

'What can we do for him?' she says and stops walking again.

'The doctor will help, I'm sure,' he says, waiting for her.

'I can't do this any more,' she says.

He lifts a hand and touches her right shoulder, then drops it. 'I agree,' he says.

She wants him to tell her she must finish what she started, not let her off the hook. She wants a fight.

They start walking again.

A group of young students in uniform approach them. The students tease and tussle with one another. One young boy holds a white cane in front of him. Reema watches as the others loiter, waiting for him without making a show of it. The children call to the boy and encourage him, coaching him to find his way. The boy with the cane passes her, his face determined and satisfied.

As they reach the curve in the road towards the doctor's office, a crowd of monks, men and women, and several foreigners come towards them, holding placards of protest as though they no longer have a use for them. They are chanting softly, heading away from the temple.

The chanting irritates her. There is no *finding peace where there is no peace*, she wants to shout. 'I don't know if I could stand life in North America,' she says instead. Why is she so intent on provocation? The truth is that in school she believed she would defy her father and find a life in his birthplace.

'Why not?'

'I don't mean that. That's something my father would like to hear me say. As a child he told me the US was full of people who were cheap, fat, and unnatural, like their food.' Yosh is a man who is not easily ruffled. She doesn't trust this yogi business; the car is not only red, the car is many colours, and the car is made in California where the people are both fat and thin, the car has wheels made in Korea, has spark plugs from Germany, batteries and software from Bangalore.

She would like to tell him about her family, how strange it is, how out of sync it is with everything Indian, everything British, everything American. She wants to tell him about her mother, how she was not a silent mother on the sidelines, but made herself appear so. She wants him to know that she is not confused at all. She is all these things and should not have to choose one. The wind brings clouds in front of the sun and the air feels damp.

'Do you like me?' he asks.

Has there been anyone else who has ever said it like this to her? There was a freckled boy in sixth form, at a dance, a small circle of light through which he walked towards her as she stood in the dark corner with her friends. She was the 'Paki' among them, the girl with green eyes but brown skin, and she watched as he approached from the light — surely to tell her so, again, like the boys who always whispered it behind her back. She was sure he was approaching to taunt her and to ask one of her friends to dance, but instead he stood in front of her and said, 'Why don't you like me?'

'I don't really know you,' Reema says. They reach the Khanna Clinic.

———

The day is full of light and heat now in the Pink House, but the doctor wears a scarf and a woollen cardigan over his kurta pyjamas. Jackson is sitting on the bed with Reema beside him. She touches his forearm to reassure him, because this doctor doesn't believe that everything is as fine as Jackson has been insisting.

'They said you felt faint,' the doctor says.

Jackson raises his arms high in the air. The doctor and the others — Yosh, Monica, Reema next to him — follow his arms with their eyes as though he will bless or curse or hypnotise them, and this makes him laugh. 'You see, I am fine now, really, I am,' he says as he lets his arms drop, his hands on the bed again, palms flat, feeling every thread of the cheap cotton sheet.

'Well, okay,' the doctor says, but reaches for his bag. 'As I'm here, I will make sure, okay?'

Amelia, he will try not to be stubborn; he will listen.

'Of course,' Jackson says. 'Thank you for coming all this way.'

The young doctor, with a full head of thick, dark hair, has smooth hands. He takes Jackson's pulse, and Jackson looks around the room at the surrounding youth. It's the hair they have in common. Hair like on dolls, and yes, Medusa, Jesus, Samson, Rapunzel — they are strong in their hair. Ha, this is something to remember. This is what the young do — tousle it, toss it, swing it in defiance. He has nearly no hair left on a body that was once hirsute. There is temple hair, Amelia, remember? Temple hair from Tirumala Venkateswara, where women shave their heads in offering to Lord Venkateswara. Temple hair is now sold all over the world, and there are celebrities with thick black manes everywhere you look. He laughs. The doctor looks up from his stethoscope. Jackson winks.

Reema catches Yosh's eye. They hold each other like this.

'Please let me see your medication,' the doctor says, drawing Reema's attention back to the bed. She fetches his toiletries bag and holds it out to the doctor, who scans the labels of the pill bottles and nods.

'I haven't taken them yet,' Jackson says, sure this is the reason for his weakness, and even as he says it he's stronger. He looks up towards the mountain. Reema was right, snow will eventually come, but not before the summer and the monsoon, and he must not spill out the tea canister just anywhere along the trail where it might be seen, might be scattered by tourists or birds or langurs.

———

He is alone with Monica on the terrace of the Pink Hotel as the sun strains to make its presence felt. He tries not to shiver, because if he shows any sign of weakness, she will report him.

'I lived in Canada as a boy,' he says. Monica has been colder to him since the doctor left. He wants to let her know that he's not a man to stay home, not a man to be frightened of anything. She looks up from her coffee and nods, gives him an indulgent smile. Yosh is talking to the hotel manager at a table at the far end of the terrace. He laughs, and this cheers Jackson. All will be well. Reema has been on the hotel computer for what feels like a long time, and he must make an effort with Monica, to let her know he's a traveller too.

There is a call from a bird in the nearby branches of the evergreen. The call is urgent but like the sucking of teeth. He stares hard at the tree and can see a small lilac-pink breast and a pink-streaked crown. A rosefinch.

'I think there are now flights from Kangra Airport to Delhi,' Monica says to Jackson, 'It might be a good idea for you to take one.' He feels stung. She looks at her watch.

He takes a sip of water. 'Yes, and in Calgary, you know, in winter, there are the Chinooks,' he says and wonders how foolish he sounds. 'I'm hardy, from those days.'

He takes another sip of water and feels the liquid going down. The doctor's hit of oxygen has given him a lift; he is strong enough to holler at the mountain in front of him to get a rise out of it, to force it to respond, to stop it from standing so smug in the face of all the empty space that will remain even after it has crumbled away or even if the sea once again rises up to cover it.

'That's not the point,' she says, finally looking into his face.

His throat tightens with the harshness of her judgement. So, that's it — that is what he will have to do. He drinks more water. If this is the way things are, he will have to make it back to Boston, because he will not be leaving Amelia here. He will take her back home, which was never quite home, but the house in which she died, and he will keep her with him a little longer. He will wait until another winter, and then perhaps he'll go out on New Year's

Eve with her in his knapsack and he will drive to Dover and will park at the entrance to the cross-country ski trails of the Noanet Woodlands. He will walk past the 24-foot-high dam and opening to the underground tailrace, where long ago stood an overshot wheel that powered the dam, and he will go towards the woods using the same path she trod weekly. Amelia loved to ski there, to marvel at the elms and the silver maples, the spruce and pine. She would tease him that he never liked to leave the trail, while she would glide off into the deep snow between the trees and slip and fall and not mind. But he will show her this time: on New Year's Eve he will go off-piste, and be a risk-taker like he never was in their marriage, and he will find the tallest elm tree in the woods and he will lie down beside it and fall asleep with her in his arms and never wake up.

He stands and Monica looks up quickly as though ready to catch him. Don't be ludicrous, he thinks.

'Going to use the facilities,' he says. 'In my day there was no sitting down in those for fear of touching the shit hole with your bottom!' He smiles to reassure her that he can still make a joke.

I am shown a photograph: boys' bodies, barely alive, on a rug, emaciated, skin scaly, dusty white, next to a mother nursing a baby, and I look away, but the other engineers tell me they are the Muslims who left for Pakistan the year before my arrival, they are telling me with satisfaction in their voices that things need to happen quickly with this dam and all the building, all the progress that must be made now that India is free and new, but all I can see in the photograph is the mark of cholera.

———

In the corridor he catches sight of Reema in profile, her head bowed, face wet with sadness. She is coming from the direction of the small office at the far end of the hotel where guests can use the computer to make international calls. He stops. She hasn't seen him. She takes the stairs in twos and peels off towards her room.

He makes his way to the small office to inspect it for its wrongs to her, because he needs to make things right before he leaves India, so that Amelia will forgive him for being a man who did not dance with her. But there is nothing in the room except phones, a fax machine and the computer. On the mahogany desk the large monitor displays the Skype icon. Amelia loved Skype. She used it weekly, to see her sister and nieces in Victoria. He sits in front of the monitor. He has an account, which he used only to speak to her when she was out west. He opens it, slowly, one poke of a key at a time. JacksonBoston. While hers is Ameliacloser. She had been so proud of it, as a woman who had travelled the world but was still sceptical about all this newfangled closeness. Close only in words cannot really be close, she would say. He opens her contact. Her last call to him was less than a year ago, from Victoria, where she was visiting for her sister's birthday. She had scolded him for forgetting to renew the fitness club membership that she'd encouraged him to make better use of. He was starting to slow down, she said, and it was important that he kept up the swimming and that she did her stretching.

Their mornings had been for reading and catching up on the news. She had an exercise class at eleven; he had the occasional round of golf or, in the winter until recently, he would get in the pool at the club, splash around and call that exercise. Their lunch would be big, with a nap afterwards, and on weekday afternoons they would make lists of the people they needed to contact to arrange the following week's activities: guests for upcoming birthdays or anniversaries; bridge partners for the weekend; health professionals for the general upkeep. They were a healthy couple, the envy of their single women friends who had lost their husbands, decades ago in some cases. They took their weekends seriously: relaxing, visiting, entertaining, and then the week would arrive and back they'd go to their schedule, as though being paid for it.

He hits the green video call button. Oh. He waits, his eyes wide. There is no ring but a voice comes on ... 'The person you are trying to reach is currently unavailable. Please leave a message ...'

The beep startles him.

He's being recorded. His heart races.

'Sweetheart. It's me ...' He looks around; no one is in earshot. He sees her in the living room, a book on her lap, her eyes closed, and knows that she will deny she was asleep if he teases her. He hears her in the kitchen, singing 'Oh What A Beautiful Morning' to the window over the sink. He smells her in the bathroom, in the sheets, on the couch. He tells a joke and it bombs; he tickles her and they laugh and laugh and laugh, until they both have to pee.

'There's a girl here — she made a choir ...'

Amelia is in bed with pneumonia and the tiny strokes have begun, and even these — these twitches that took her away from him a few cells at a time — these he misses because they were hers and hers alone. His tears splash boldly onto the keyboard. 'Where are you?' There is the low machine hiss of recording. The photo of Amelia on her Skype account is coy, her head tilted gently left, an attempt to hide the extra skin at her chin that began to show around the time of the photo was taken, when she was trying new technology, still up for everything. His wife's vanity arouses him.

'Where are you?'

Nineteen

The door of her room clicks shut as Reema walks to the curtains, draws them open to the mountain and unlatches the window to swing it out. She steps back and throws herself onto the bed.

She dries her eyes. She hates him. What is it that she must know? How an economy fails, when the valley will flood, where the cows go to die, who will find the slipper of the dead man in the street, why the monkeys slide their backsides along the stones, how to breathe through cellophane and stay away from the top floors of buildings? She flings the pillow off the bed. How dare he pressure her. The mountain and its snow-capped peak is cocky in its certainty about all there is to know. There is a solution in two words: mifepristone, misoprostol — one little pill after the other. Mifepristone first, return to the clinic two days later for the misoprostol. *Mi, mi, mi,* she would sing, like Tosca.

She gets up out of bed, tucks her T-shirt into her skirt. She should be wearing a shalwar kameez. The last time she did was at Jyoti and Aditya's engagement party in London, where she felt like an imposter. As a child her mother helped her to play dress-up by putting her in saris, but her father objected, insisting she dress like an English girl and telling her she was not to concern herself with frills and flowers. She clears her throat. Dhurpad music requires a vocal range over two octaves. Trained in western music for so many

159

years, Reema's chest voice can manage this range; she has no need to resort to head tones. Facing the window and the mountain she places her hands on her hips. To sing clearly in aakaar — vowels over consonants — she will need speed. If she starts in sargam, as Sadhana taught her, she will slowly be able to slide into aakaar. *Sa sa ni sa sa ni dha ni sa. Aa aa aa …*

Do you think we should tell anyone else? Robert had said on the Skype call. When did her body become *we*?

She said *of course not* and added a smile, to assure him that it being their secret still made it all the more precious. He paused or the screen froze. 'Can you hear me?' she said, again and again. When the screen moved again he was shaking his head in disbelief. They went on to talk about the weather in London, what she'd done since the wedding, the rock that had hit Jackson's head, the temple statues, the mountains, even the dry humour of the Indian transport signs. She didn't mention Yosh, no name attached to 'our driver' and no way in which she could have described to Robert that Yosh's 'Do you like me?' meant more to her than anything Robert had said in months.

Sa ni dha pa dha ni sa … she sings. She moves closer to the window and hears her voice echo. She closes the window firmly.

'Reema,' Robert said after the tiny bandages of small talk, 'I need to know what my life is going to be. You must know.' The screen flickered. The connection dropped out a few seconds later and she didn't try to get it back.

… aa aa aa aa aa aa aa.

She tries another line of sargam, emphasising the consonants this time. She sings louder.

A gentle knock at her door stops her. She goes to open it, and when she sees who it is, she stiffens.

'Nothing like a song to chase away the blues,' Jackson says, holding his hand up to the sky to feel for rain. It wasn't a joke, Amelia, he's not making jokes; he's trying to help. He puts his hand in his pocket and raises his eyebrows at her.

'Are you sure you should be out of bed?'

'Feeling much better,' Jackson says. He looks inside her room. He wants to see something that will convince him that a young woman crying behind doors is not the end of the world. Where is the girl's mother? 'I wanted to thank you for getting the doctor,' he says, 'but I'm really fine, adjusting to the altitude. The little hit of oxygen sorted me out.' There is suspicion in her eyes, and he scrambles to find something that will take it away. He doesn't want to be a burden. 'I could run up the mountain today!' he says, but this has the opposite of the effect he was aiming for.

Her brow creases. 'I've had enough of that,' she says.

'No, I don't mean — '

In the pixelated Skype version of Robert, his chin was wobbly, just like Jackson's.

'I could treat you all to dinner and we could talk about the next leg of our adventure,' Jackson says. *Guldasta*: it means bouquet. They used to call Mrs Bhandari that. Full, generous: this is what he's aiming for.

Adventure. She holds herself in. *Lord of the Rings, Lord of the Flies* ... like flies, she thinks, like flies to ... And there —the image of a body bobbing in the flooded reservoir — a foot, a finger, a head. She tries to shake it. The notes she was singing before he interrupted her had been making her calmer. Now this.

'Haven't you put us through enough?' Her tone is harsh, but really why must she now care for this old white man like a child. His face falls with regret; she resists the cascade of guilt. 'What more do you want from me?' she asks, more gently.

What rises between them feels like barbed wire.

He widens his eyes so that they do not water. Amelia accused him of not being able to stay the course of an argument, never facing her when she was upset, instead padding off down to the basement to read engineering magazines or follow the traces of the leak along the ceiling from the bathroom pipes that he refused to have someone else fix.

'I'm sorry. You're right,' he says. And there ... *there is the woman in the alley, and she is screaming*. He reaches out his hand to Reema.

'Please,' she says, and makes a shooing motion.

'I didn't mean to anger you,' he says. 'I am grateful for all you've done.' He turns from her, shuffling down the hall because his feet are thick with fluid, the water pills not doing their job today.

———

Out of the hotel and onto the road. Reema has no idea which direction to take. Two monks pass in front of her heading towards the centre of town. The road is quiet, with very few vehicles, and she wants noise. She looks around. To her left, the density of shops diminishes; to her right, the shops are open, but quiet. She follows the monks, past a Japanese restaurant, a western bakery, and small shops selling shawls, hats, more shops with soap, detergent, and rows and rows of small packets of peanuts pinned up one under the other. The monks walk so slowly that they seem to be in pain. Their saffron robes are paired with capes of the same material, and one monk has wrapped his around his neck up to his ears like a scarf. She passes them. On the other side of the road, approaching her, are two elderly Tibetan women in traditional dress. One wears an apron with pink, blue, green, and mustard stripes. The colourful pattern of this woman's apron is a sign that she is married — a small fact from Monica's guidebooks. Over their dresses both women wear quilted down jackets. Their faces are wide, brown, placid.

Reema sees Yosh coming towards her down the hill, a little behind the two Tibetan women. He is absorbed in his own thoughts. His hair flies loose; his face is oblivious to the possibility of being observed. His arms swing like they know joy, but she has never seen this in him up close; she wonders if joy can live on its own in the body, undetected.

'Hello,' she calls.

He catches her eye, comes towards her, self-consciously.

'Where are you going?' he says, as he reaches her.

'Nowhere, really.'

He pushes his hair behind his left ear. She imagines him as young boy, watching his father cry with pride upon returning to his village in a BMW.

'Actually, I was looking for you,' she says. *We're in this together*, Robert said on Skype. But she has never felt so lonely in her life. 'Do you want to go for a walk?'

'Yes.'

They make their way through the centre of town and head towards its limits, following signs to Dal Lake. At the turn-off to the lake there is a road in the lee of a mountain, with woods on both sides. They pass a road sign that reads: 'Himachal Police Welcomes You. Divorce Speed Not Wife.'

She laughs. No, divorce your wife and set her free. Her shoulders relax. This air, this light, yes.

When they arrive at St John in the Wilderness Church at the base of the mountain's slope, they haven't spoken again, but their hands brush at the entrance to the grounds, where the date above the arched gate reads 1852, and she notes how young this church is in this ancient country. A few tourists flow in the cathedral doors, a few out, and she leaves Yosh at the gates to walk towards the entrance. She looks into the church from the doorway and feels the cool air from the modest interior. The voices around her are soft, nearly whispers. She takes in all she needs to see and turns to leave, when she sees Yosh outside, talking to Monica.

Joining them, she touches Monica's arm in greeting. The three of them stand silently, the question of Jackson hanging heavily in the air.

'I'm sorry,' Reema says. The other two nod.

'We need to get him home,' Monica says. She is as gentle as she was on the mountain, but also clear and firm.

'Yes,' Reema says.

'You can take him,' Monica says.

'Yes,' she says nodding. Of course. 'I'll call my family in Palampur, tell them I can't make it.'

'You shouldn't have to ...' Monica says.

'I know, but ...'

Yosh says, 'No. I'll drive you both — Jackson to the airport, you to Palampur.'

Monica sighs. 'This guy has roamed the world his whole life and has taken everything for granted, and he's still doing that.' She gathers up her bag, her sweater, and prepares to walk off.

'I can take him on my own,' Reema says. Monica's plans with Yosh have meaning for her, the opposite of banking, and Yosh has need of work. They were set to see Shimla, to follow Siddhartha's path, to trace a journey that might allow for change and insight, while all Reema has been looking for is some kind of sign. Come, monkey.

Yosh's expression objects, but then he nods, capitulating.

'I will make bookings,' Reema says, 'and Jackson can fly from Kangra to Delhi.' That way the only car they will need is one to get them down the mountain.

Monica adjusts the strap of the camera around her neck. 'Okay, I'll meet you later,' she says to Yosh, who nods in agreement.

Monica leaves them. The scent of vanilla from her shampoo remains in the air.

'I'm sorry,' Reema says, again, but Yosh does not acknowledge her apology or the need for one as they continue on their walk.

The pine trees have cones the size of small creatures, like squirrels hanging from the branches. These northern trees, northern smells, northern sounds. Reema has another distant cousin her mother has told her about. This cousin is known as the fearless one — a woman who works in health care and moved to Ladakh to work for the World Health Organisation. This cousin has been battling to end tuberculosis among the Tibetan refugee community and works seven days a week in a hospital. What would it be like to battle for something so important? Reema only has to keep an old, helpless man alive, and to think about how the world must change.

'Let's go back,' she says to Yosh. Suddenly there's no time to waste.

On the road back into town another road sign makes her smile: 'Go Slowly and Enjoy the Scenery. Don't Go Slowly and Join the Scenery.'

TWENTY

Men wrapped head to ankle in muslin, bedrolls on their heads, children on their shoulders holding cooking pots, their faces black with dirt. Hundreds, one after the other, walking towards, no, walking away from burning streets. A war correspondent took this photo, the dam engineers told me, but the fighting is over now, the Muslims in muslin are gone, and this is Life, *one of them said, and laughed and the other said* Magazine, *ha ha, and I laughed along like a fake joker in their gang and they told me I was safe to walk the Amritsar night streets back to my lodgings at Mrs Bhandari's guest house. I must have been drunk to see what I saw, they said the next day, I must have been, because the fighting has stopped, they said, it's safe here now. But I saw the men circle the woman. They circled her. Her scream was cut off. And the lines and lines of men, women and children in muslin and dirt repeated in my mind like a photograph of white birds, egrets of pain.*

TWENTY-ONE

On the walk back, Yosh describes his first yoga teacher, Prakash — also the name of Reema's grandfather, the one who fell from a ladder, she tells him, before she becomes aware that they are on more personal ground now. The yogi master had been old when Yosh first went to him. A master of note, he taught only those he chose himself, in the one small room of his lodgings in Dharamkot. Yosh had found him by visiting the same chai stand every day to listen to the local men discussing village issues. He begged Prakash to take him on and had to convince him he was worthy of his time by telling him stories of New York every afternoon when Prakash came for chai. Prakash was a Buddhist, and in Yosh's home state of Maharashtra many Dalits had rejected their caste by converting to Buddhism. Prakash wanted to know why a Dalit would want to do yoga. Yosh spoke to him for hours about Ambedkar, a politician from Maharashtra who opposed caste, who wanted Dalits like himself to succeed. And this was exactly what his father pursued. But when Yosh moved to America he learned that success is stupid. Success is about being a white man. In America he could do as he pleased but this brought him nothing. Now he wanted to disappear inside his own body so that no one had any say over him. Only by hearing details of a life he would never lead and being assured that Yosh was finished with it, would Prakash agree to teach him anything.

Reema is dragging out the walk back from the church, resisting her sense of duty to Jackson. She has tried to keep her questions interesting so that Yosh will talk more about himself. She needs to know how to be in the world as it is, now — designed to be broken in a crash, designed to cause pain. Prakash is dead now, Yosh says. But a first master is always a first. Prakash taught Yosh how to walk on the outside edges of his feet whenever he became anxious. To walk for an hour on the edges of his feet would bring him better balance. Monica's story of the ghost with backwards feet trying to walk forward was about longing, while this walking on edges is meant to be soothing. She tries it, but it's impossible at this pace.

'The old man's legs are swollen,' Yosh says, suddenly.

'And?'

'I'm not a doctor, but swelling in the legs is a bad sign. A heart that's not pumping well causes fluids to build up, leading to shortness of breath. I don't know if he should be on a plane.'

She looks at him for a long moment. Now what should she do with the old man?

Ahead of them, coming around the road's sloping curve, is a shepherd and his entire herd of goats, trundling along, guided by the careful movement of his staff. The shepherd has a patterned wool blanket strapped to his back, and a white shawl draped awkwardly around his neck. The shawl looks fat and sinewy, and one side of it hangs lower than the other. The shepherd's herd trundles to the right and then the left, in response to a honk from a jeep. Two cars pass. As Reema gets closer, the goats skitter and bleat, and their hooves click along the road. Run away, goat.

The shepherd calls something to his herd and Reema hears the shawl on his shoulders utter a tiny, hungry bleat. Now she sees the kid, its red eyes, the triangle nose and front hoof — so clearly not a shawl but a small, tired creature that the shepherd carries across his shoulders like the favourite child.

'They are Gaddi, people of this valley,' Yosh explains. 'They take their herds over the Indrahar Pass in the summer, to Chamba, to Lahaul and Spiti.'

She watches the slow, light gait of the shepherd who manoeuvres his herd, takes this part of his day for what it is, with the traffic and the injured or ill kid around his neck, ever watchful with the left right left of his staff. She tries the edges of her feet again.

'Over the pass we'd see snow,' he says.

But she is tired of the idea of snow.

'The Gaddi are renowned for their stories,' Yosh adds.

The shepherd and his kid cape make a pair she has never seen before. He advances his goats with a precise yet calm swing of his arm, a method honed over millennia. The kid bleats in response to the others among the herd, which seem to converse about tiny, imperceptible dangers in the road.

'Last year in a storm there was lightning and thunder, even without rain. It went on for twenty hours. A Gaddi shepherd was struck by lightning and killed. Along with thirty of his goats.'

'Thirty?' she says.

'Yes, three zero.'

'That's not possible.'

'Well, I don't know.'

'How can lightning strike thirty goats and a shepherd all at once?'

'Maybe they were huddled together ...'

There is noise — honking and loud shouting come from the bus depot at the entrance to McLeodganj. She looks to see a crowd forming.

'Maybe the bolt travelled through them — they acted as conductors to one another,' Yosh says.

'No ...' She shakes her head, smiling all the while.

The crowd is growing at the bus depot.

'Maybe they didn't want their shepherd to leave them alone,' Yosh says, also smiling.

Now they can see men rushing towards the commotion near where cars, vans, and off-duty taxis are parked.

A car backfires, the bang making them both start, but then there is another, and another, and it is not a car but a gun. The parking lot is now a riot of running men. Yosh holds his arm out in front of Reema to stop her from moving. She grabs his forearm and he allows this touch for a few short seconds before glancing at her to make sure she will stay still. Then he walks ahead to get a better look. Army officers in fatigues have their guns raised, and a group of men in tracksuits are being subdued by the men surrounding them.

'It really was guns?' Reema calls after him.

'The soldiers have shot into the air to scare them off, that's all,' he says. He gestures that everything is fine, and he keeps walking towards the centre of town. She follows. 'For some reason this is a favourite place for young Israelis to hang out,' he says. 'They come here after they finish their military service. They go crazy, do drugs.'

He seems casual about the gunfire. She wonders if Yosh has ever done drugs, blown off steam, gone crazy.

'Indians are asking the government to stop their visas,' he says.

In the central square, a group of Japanese tourists is gathered, listening to their tour guide. As if to prove Yosh's point, two young Israeli men run past them, sideswiping one of the Japanese men, who wobbles, then catches his balance and smiles at himself for his quick recovery. He nods and nods and smiles, at the guide and the others in the group, saying okay, okay in his language, okay nothing serious as he continues to nod.

As she and Yosh carry on down Jogiwara Road, Reema notices a shopkeeper rushing to secure the wares in the front of his shop, rearranging boxes to make tighter angles of pots piled on each other, pushing other pans and boxes of utensils into the corners of his display tables as though preparing for a storm. His movements are urgent and determined. Groups of people begin to walk faster, or is she imagining this? Is everything more urgent? Something is always on the verge of happening but rarely does, she thinks, calming herself, until she looks up and sees Jackson coming towards them, leaning into the slope of the street. She runs to him.

'What are you doing?'

Jackson tries to read the mood on her face, doesn't want to anger her again. *The scream in the alley.* He needs to keep going. The canister is secure in his backpack. This is a town of temples, of holiness, and a spiritual leader people come from all over the world to see. This place is something to be shared with Amelia, even though he's decided not to leave her here. He touches Reema's arm to reassure her he's not doing anything foolish. He says, 'Just out for some air.'

'But you are not well enough for this.' She waves her hand towards the people in the street.

'Let's sit and have chai,' says Yosh, coming up behind her. He looks up and down the road for a suitable spot.

'I don't need chai — I need air,' Jackson says. He wonders where the two of them have been. A man with scars like Yosh's should not be alone with a young woman.

'But you weren't well,' Reema says.

How can he describe for them what goes on inside him — how he can feel suddenly like a man of forty: how from time to time he thinks that if Amelia were alive he would have no complaints other than some stiffness and the need to pee too often. He looks into Reema's uncomprehending face. Of course, Amelia, he must be gracious. 'Yes, chai, great.'

When they enter the small café, Jackson sits down and immediately remembers the taste of a cake he has thought of only now. The Tibetan woman who comes to their table has the bright face of someone he knew long ago.

'Cardamom cake!' he blurts. 'I once had a cardamom cake in this town. Do you have any of that?' When the woman apologises over her lack of cardamom cake and offers alternatives, Jackson doesn't mind, satisfied with the memory alone. He asks the woman where her family is, how many children she has, what the winter was like for them. She speaks English with difficulty but answers each question, looking pleased with his efforts to make conversation. She excuses herself at last to make the tea.

'You see? There are so many people you know,' he says to his companions. 'You just have to meet them first.' He sits back in exhaustion, making sure to keep an eye on Yosh and the hand that rests on the table, close to Reema's.

Reema sips just once, watching outside as people continue to rush by. The chai is too sweet for her.

Several young men in woollen caps run by the window, one of them with two crates of oranges on his shoulders, trying to ensure they don't spill out. 'What do you think is happening?' she asks Yosh.

'I'm not sure,' Yosh says. 'Over the years, there have been some confrontations between the Tibetans and Indians, but nothing too big.'

She needs to know more about these things he refers to so casually. 'What confrontations?'

'Several years ago — on one of my first trips back home — an Indian taxi driver killed a Tibetan man,' Yosh says.

'Did he go to jail?'

'Yes. And then there were retaliations, vandalism, some fighting. It became clear that many Indians were having trouble with the refugees starting their own businesses.'

'Go on,' she says. He doesn't continue proudly, the way a storyteller will to hold his audience, drawing them deeper. He is tentative.

'Many of the Tibetans believed that it was Chinese plotters who killed the man, so that the town of McLeodganj and all its people would turn against them and make them go home.'

'Yes, I think so,' Jackson says, then hears his nonsense and shakes his head — he knows nothing of this.

'In the end the Dalai Lama announced that if his presence and his people were responsible for this violence, he would have to think seriously about moving — building a community outside of Dharmsala where there would be peace.'

Reema's eyes are fixed on Yosh's hands.

'A few days later the taxi drivers' union and other associations of Indians in Dharmsala asked for an audience with His Holiness. They begged him not to leave, not to take the Tibetans anywhere else, and promised cooperation.'

Jackson takes a sip of tea. *Their arms in the air, yes, like they are chasing demons or they are men wanting wings.*

'Now and then there are small scuffles, but nothing more,' Yosh says.

Jackson places the cup on the table, taking care to hold it steady, so as not to reveal that his hands are shaky.

'It's not like in the valley at Pong Dam, not like when they let the dam out. I told you so,' Jackson says and looks at Reema, defiantly. 'I told you that it wasn't the fault of the engineers on the dam, because they do not control these things. The people who drowned, they had refused …' He catches himself. He has lost track of what he is saying. The faces of the others at his table are familiar, but he's not sure of their names. Their eyes are full of concern. 'Yes, yes,' he says and wipes his brow. 'I think I read that in the newspaper.' He lifts his backpack from the floor beside the table and when he hears the canister move inside he is brought back to this café and these companions.

Reema and Yosh exchange a look, and Yosh raises his eyebrows, saying with them, again, that she must do something about this old man.

'I will head back to Delhi soon, Jackson,' she says, making room for him to say that he will join her.

'Yes, yes,' he says. Proving that he's back from that inexact borderland he's been straddling, he asks, 'What about Palampur? Your folks.' He nudges her arm. 'All that tea to drink! And all those tunes you must teach them to sing.'

'I will visit them another time. I'm going to look for flights from Kangra Airport instead of Amritsar, so that Yosh can head off with Monica to Manali as planned. You can come with me.'

In Boston by now the snow has turned to slush, and it will not suit his purpose. It will be dirty and melting. The air will be damp and the tease of false spring will go on for weeks and weeks.

'What? You've come all this way and you won't see your family? Nonsense. As for me, I love tea! And there's nothing a large extended family likes more than an old man to amuse them.'

He winks, at her and Yosh, but feels a stab of shame.

TWENTY-TWO

At her window, Reema watches a short, elderly woman in thick burgundy shalwar, a red cardigan and a floral apron climb up the hill from the valley carrying a big bundle on her back. The woman's hair is streaked with grey, her face lined, but her body is strong. Hunched over from the weight — a load of firewood that is nearly the size of the woman herself — she stops to sip water from a plastic bottle. The water must be fetched, the wood too. Reema steps back from the window and begins to collect her belongings from around the room.

She hears Monica singing next door. A low chant like a monk's. Monica would make a fine monk. She would be dutiful, stolid, and, like the female monks in town whose shaved skulls curve towards their necks like a talisman to rub, her apparent vulnerability would be her strength. She might become like the woman who carries wood on her back, and she might make her way up the mountain, tired yet strong. Work and sleep belong to everyone. Or at least they should.

The most recent of her father's clippings from the *Hindustan Times* details the plague of suicides among young Dalit men. Several have committed suicide at their universities — one recently in Hyderabad, another at the All India Institute of Medical Sciences. These young men hanged themselves in their dorm rooms, the first leaving a note that said his birth had been a fatal accident.

Love, work, sleep. For everyone.

She unzips the knapsack and starts to place her things in it. On the shelf beside the bed are books left by other travellers. *The Tibetan Book of the Dead*; *Sons and Daughters of Buddha*; *The Handbook of Tibetan Buddhist Symbols*. She considers taking one.

She hears Monica's door open and close, then there is a knock on hers.

'How it's going?' Monica says.

'Okay,' Reema says. She points towards the bed. 'Have a seat,' she says, and sits herself.

Monica hesitates then comes to sit beside her.

'I'm nearly packed, but I'm slow, tired all the time these days,' Reema says.

Monica nods. 'Still jet-lagged?'

'No, I don't think so.' Some days there is nothing different; other days there is a mild ache, everywhere — her head, her back, her breasts. 'It's something else.'

Monica gestures for her to say more.

Reema shifts her weight and sits straighter. The noise of a drill, or saw, a high-pitched machine, begins to wail through the open window. She glances at Monica's knees. Solid, confident knees. The drill reaches a higher pitch. 'I didn't think it would be so busy in the mountains,' she says. They sit in silent agreement.

'London's crazy busy,' Monica says. She shakes her head, 'I don't know how you live there.' Someone down the hall calls and a child answers. Reema searches the room for something to say.

'I didn't want you to think I'm cold-hearted or anything,' Monica says.

'How do you mean?'

'You did a good thing with the old man, a kind thing,' Monica says. 'I liked Triund in the end — never thought I'd see monkeys.'

'Jackson's something, right?' Reema says. She wants to be angrier with him, but a part of her is in awe of an old man who still has the passion to do something outrageous. She knows men her own age who do nothing but get on the tube at 7 a.m. from Monday to Friday, work all day, drink all evening and watch sports together with their mates, sharing stories of their meaningless triumphs. They are proud potential CEOs, husbands, fathers — proud of their future retirements, their future irrelevance. When she dies, will Robert travel across the world to sprinkle her remains? 'So stubborn,' she says.

Monica furrows her brow, then smiles. 'I never met either of my grandfathers,' she says. 'My mother's father disowned my mum for being loose and having black friends. My father's father died a long time ago, in New York. I have a few great-uncles on my dad's side, who know Jyoti's family,' she says. 'Old people make me tense.'

If this is true, what kind of holiday has Monica had? There's Jackson, but there are also the old men sleeping by the roadside, the old women on the mountain with loads strapped to their backs — so many old faces in this country.

'My mother has said, my whole life, "Don't worry, one day you'll be just like me, and old ..." but I won't. I'm sure I won't,' Reema says.

'You won't?'

'I mean, I will, but I won't be like *her*.'

They sit in silence again. The mountain. The furnishings.

An unlit candle. The drill has stopped, and there is no shouting in the hotel.

There is a nearly imperceptible movement towards each other. Monica raises her hand and lays it along Reema's jaw, barely touching it and it's as though they will kiss. Reema closes her eyes. When Monica's hand drops away, she opens them again. They readjust themselves on the bed, reeling in the desire whose source must surely be loss — of control, of grandparents, of jobs, of hope.

'I do know what you mean,' Monica says softly.

Reema stands, missing the hand on her face, and begins to pick up the clothing littered around the room. 'Have you ever had an abortion?' she says, glancing over her shoulder at Monica.

'What?'

Reema catches the startled look on Monica's face before turning back to her clothes. 'Just wondered.'

During her first year at music college, her best friend, Ruth, had had two. Reema had accompanied her to one, at the Marie Stopes Clinic, and Ruth's boyfriend went along to the other. It seemed as normal as going to the dentist. Ruth came out the same as she went in. Reema turns to Monica, who gently shakes her head.

———

He sits on his suitcase to force it shut — the zip reluctant, the suitcase always too small. Amelia had the smallest suitcases of any woman he'd ever encountered while travelling. She taught him to pack lightly, to take only what is necessary. She is the only thing necessary now. He doesn't need both pieces of luggage. He opens the zip and takes out trousers, a shirt, jacket, the dress shoes he wore at the wedding, a sweater, a rain jacket. Removing the tea canister from the backpack he places it in the centre of the suitcase and readjusts the few remaining items around it to keep it secure. He zips the suitcase closed again.

The photo of the fleeing men, arms in the air — this was not all the accountant at the dam showed me. He sat on a rock and drew a picture of a circumcised penis and told me that a Hindu mob stripped a fourteen-year-old boy naked to confirm he was circumcised, threw him into a pond and held down his head with bamboo poles, while a Bengali engineer educated in England noted on his Rolex watch the time it took for the boy to drown and wondered how tough the life of a Muslim bastard was. But how did he know, this accountant? How did the man know what the Bengali engineer had thought? Or the shape of circumcision?

Twenty-Three

As Jackson lies on his bed, suitcase packed, ready to leave, he discovers a new opening in time. The more vivid these borderless moments have become, the more he realises he can slip into them without moving. This opening is to the present, but it is a hundred miles away at the Pong Dam where he is standing with Mike.

This morning a blue-throated barbet became tangled in the netting around the fig tree. Mike spent several minutes with the tiny body clutched in his hand, its nearly neon feathers ruffled and shooting up through his fingers while its black-and-yellow beak pecked at them. Jackson held the shears and clipped the netting in four places before they could release the bird. Now Jackson watches for the barbet in the distant trees. It will come back; its kin have been caught before. Mike will search for finer netting to surround the tree.

The last wedding guests are packing their suitcases into the Tata SUV and Jackson thinks he spots the blue, green and red feathers on the other side of the garden. Jyoti's mother and father wave. The last cousin gets into the front seat next to the driver and closes the door.

The retreat season will start now. Mike will tell each of the yoga groups about the garden — the names of the plants, their place of origin, the fruit trees' annual yield.

He and Jackson will need to drive into Talwara for supplies —
cooking oil, toilet paper, salt. But not just yet. Jackson watches out
for the barbet.

TWENTY-FOUR

Low clouds hang over the mountains, closing in the town. Jackson is cold. He stands in the street, touching the icy metal of the handle on the jeep door. He grabs it more firmly, but Yosh is suddenly beside him, blocking the way to the driver's seat.

'I've put some water and sandwiches in the back for you,' Yosh says.

The young man has been a stellar guide and interpreter, so what is still unnerving about him? The scars on his back, the knowingness of his silence, the silence in his knowing.

'I used to drive across America,' Jackson says. Amelia, it's okay, I'll behave. 'Thank you, that's kind,' he says, and he releases the handle, resigning himself to the back seat.

'I need to sort out things with the hotel. Back soon,' Yosh says and returns to the lobby.

In Brazil, in Zimbabwe, in the Punjab, Jackson had drivers, while Mrs Bhandari drove herself and others back and forth across the border between India and Pakistan. Only when he took an office job at the Massachusetts Water Authority did he need to drive himself anywhere. Amelia was always a better driver, but he is still a pro. Safe. Stamina for long trips. He watches as Monica lifts her heavy suitcase into the boot. She slams it shut and stands beside the back door, waiting for the others.

'How was lunch?' Jackson says to her through the back passenger window.

She doesn't respond. That's okay. He closes his eyes and his head dips forward. He hears sounds around him, but they come from above the surface of something he is beneath.

'Am I late?' Reema says when she arrives. Her cousin had kept her on the phone.

'We're still waiting for Yosh,' Monica says.

'Right,' says Reema. When she catches Monica's eye, her face is impossible to read; they both look away.

'You take the front,' Reema says, as she puts her backpack in the boot.

———

Jackson opens his eyes as they get underway; his vision feels sharp but his ears seem plugged. The jeep winds down the road slowly, the main street of the town more crowded even than yesterday. At the curve beyond the Nikon sign, between the Tibetan Mini Mart and the Himalayan Pharmacy, there is a small chai stand. Yosh pulls over to the side of the road, where a cow rummages in a high pile of rubbish — plastic bottles, egg cartons, juice containers, foil crisp packets and peanuts bags. An old man sits on a small stool near the road's edge. His face is like a dry riverbed, cracked where rivulets used to run, his beard white, his eyes still bright. Jackson thinks that this man, hunched over a small table with two empty cups in front of him, must be a Gaddi from Ghera or one of the villages higher up in the mountain.

'I'm sorry, just a small stop, someone I know ...' Yosh says. Even to Jackson, the slam of his door is loud. He watches as Yosh squats beside the old man, whose round woollen cap has a traditional geometric woven pattern. Yosh listens intently to the man, his head bowed, as he adjusts his squat to rest on one knee. Jackson's eyes close.

'Forgive me, but I won't see him again,' Yosh says when he slides once more into the driver's seat. Open and close, up and down, Jackson's eyes open again.

'Your friend,' Jackson says. 'How old is he?'

'I don't know,' Yosh says as he puts the jeep in gear and pulls out. 'In his mid-nineties I think. I met him when I first came here, but old people don't always have a specific date for their birthdays, just a vague idea. Even my father's generation is not as precise as we are now. My friend's mother counted cows and seasons but didn't pay attention to a calendar.'

Jackson sees him check in the rear-view mirror to see if Reema has been listening.

———

The road to Palampur winds over a bridge that crosses a river in the valley, where it is now drier and hotter. Jackson is awake to the road signs — one that tells him they have crossed the Baner Khad River. He is awake to the sound of large trucks carrying oil and grain, to the tanks and pumps of petrol stations on the outskirts of a small village, to main streets with vegetable stalls and sweet vendors. As they descend and the mountains grow shorter behind them, the clouds cling to the peaks, while in the valley there is blue sky. The atmosphere in the jeep has changed. Amelia, there is new knowledge between these young people.

The jeep follows a local bus that stops and starts. After a time, Yosh passes it at speed. All the honking, jolting, all the turning and the near sideswiping of pedestrians, all the cows in the middle, on the side, on each other, and the beep-beeping that they are oblivious to — honking to say *here I am, I'm coming, don't mind me, I am overtaking you, thank you*. All of this, as a young man, he used to love, but today he misses the I-90 outside of Boston, which could take him to Cleveland, Billings, Spokane and eventually Seattle — all the way across a country with barely a bend in the road.

He closes his eyes. 'Florida,' he says, but the word comes from a decade ago.

'There's so much you don't see,' Amelia had said after making her way through the pages of the Florida retirement community brochure he had handed her as a surprise. Then she corrected herself, 'No, that you don't *want* to see.'

What is he to do with this now? Did he see her sniff the maid's neck for a trace of her own perfume? Is she gone because of something he didn't want to see?

He opens his eyes. The jeep is soaring alongside a riverbed that has only a trickle of water in a thin line between dry rocks and boulders. He closes his eyes again.

Her legs were long, still muscular, and in the winter their grip was more intent, pulling him deeper. Bulky sweaters, long johns, even hats to bed on January nights and you, oh. They made love more often in the winter, and even when his fingers got twisted with arthritis, her back more hunched, winter was not her issue; it was his. It wasn't the mini-strokes that took her away at all; it was his infinitesimal yet perpetual neglect of who she really was.

I have only a meagre understanding of the language, so I cannot know exactly what the man is saying, cannot be certain of anything, as I walk quickly back to Mrs Bhandari's, but the men in the kurta pyjamas are laughing and I think one is saying he has drawn the short stick, because he has to fuck her even though she is now dead.

———

They have slowed and Jackson is awake again. There is a crowd on both sides of the jeep as it crawls along the road with just enough room for one car in one direction. A fair, a festival. The honking is unbearable, on top of the drums and voices.

Carnival, Trinidad, a stopover with my father, on our way back to Calgary from Venezuela. Whistles and steel pans and the bouncing bottoms of the women I pretend not to see.

'The build-up to Holi,' Yosh says. 'A fair.'

Reema watches the back of Yosh's head and imagines him as a young boy at these festivities. She has secretly loved Holi her whole life — secretly, because her father would ruin it for them every year, telling them over and over of the one Holi he spent in Uttar Pradesh, when some Chamar boys in a village nearby turned a man of a higher caste blue and red. The man retaliated by burning forty-two Dalit houses to the ground. Nothing to celebrate, he would say.

But there are photos of her as a baby at a fair like this: fried sweets, pinwheels and a small Ferris wheel the height of the smallest bungalow on the road in north London where they had moved soon after.

She stares out of her window at the blankets, sari fabrics, kurtas, metal lunch boxes, wicker chairs, shawls of all lengths and thicknesses and all kinds of prints. Women try on shawls, wrapping them around their shoulders with a u-shaped dip in front. She looks up front at Monica, to see if she has noticed that these shawls are not meant to keep the neck warm; they are meant to dip just below it to cover the breasts, to ensure modesty and chastity.

Four men carry a carpet-covered bier through the bazaar on their shoulders, bearing a flower-decked statue of Lord Shiva. Women, men and children carry twigs — some twigs are painted yellow and red; others are yet to be painted. They carry the yellow and red twigs in bamboo baskets, with jaggery, vermillion powder and thread. She looks for animals. Her mother speaks of festivals where goats, pigeons, roosters, ducks, and swine are slaughtered for Gadhimai. She sees a small monkey perched on the edge of a stall that sells hats.

The monkeys in the forest of Triund were as big as some of the children she teaches at the junior academy on Saturdays, but these ones in the valley are small, like pets. She would prefer to be on the mountain, with the langurs, who are wild, free, and unafraid.

A hot breeze blows into the jeep. Her clothing is stained and smelly. The distant cousins they are headed towards are rich. Her auntie is modern, but wears silk saris that she gets custom-made in Delhi. She wears them all day long, even at home alone, or so it seemed on their Skype calls over the last few months.

A man sticks his hand through the back window, offering a wrapped sweet; another throws marigolds through it. Some petals hit Jackson, and he opens his eyes, confused. 'My brother has been trying to call,' he says, then leans back on the headrest and falls asleep again.

Reema hits the switch to close the window, then adjusts the things surrounding Jackson — his jacket, her scarf, a bottle of water. She pulls her knapsack closer, to give him space. She organises the next few hours in her mind. Her family in Palampur have a magnificent operation, the best tea in India, they claim, so they should be able to handle the old man she is bringing with her. Perhaps, after she's put Jackson on a plane, she will have one extra day on her own to think. Her organising begins to extend beyond hours, or days. Perhaps she can work for the tea company, squat in the fields on the hillside with a basket strapped to her back, picking the greenest leaves, making a place for herself. Work and sleep belong to everyone. She cleans up the marigold petals, lowers the window again and tosses them out.

Robert's lower teeth are tea-stained in places, and crooked. When she first caught herself noticing this, she felt she might not be in love with him. What would take over from love? Falling out of love is a disaster. She stares at the back of Yosh's head, his long straight black hair. She puts her arms around herself for comfort. She listens for it, but there is nothing inside her to tell her a single thing.

The jeep crosses a small bridge, built on top of one that has been washed out by a mudslide. The new bridge is made of concrete and feels strong and steady. Once they are away from the festival grounds, the traffic speeds up. She glances up in time to meet Yosh's eyes in the rear-view mirror. She looks away, out the window, at the ordered expanse of tea fields beyond the river.

———

A sound like a trumpet call comes from Jackson's mouth. He has been sleeping long enough.

'Jackson?' Reema says. 'Jackson, wake up now …' She touches his arm, and finds it hot and clammy. 'He's sweating.'

Yosh pulls onto the shoulder, the cars that were behind them honking as they pass.

'Jackson, are you okay?' Reema says, feeling his forehead. He is not okay. He seems to have a fever and his breathing is uneven. She looks to the other two for reassurance, saying, 'He's not okay.' Yosh puts the car into gear and they pull quickly back into the dance of vehicles, Yosh driving faster now, overtaking buses, flashing by the cows and pedestrians.

'Can we find a hospital?' Monica asks.

Yosh checks the mirror again and nods at Reema. He drives aggressively, passing a Tata taxi with a large family crammed in the back seat. She keeps her hand on Jackson's forehead, and, as traffic begins to slow near Palampur, Yosh pulls off the road again at a row of shops, an ATM, and an electronics merchant. Jackson opens his eyes.

'Jackson,' Reema says and takes his hand. 'How are you doing?'

'Not good,' he says.

'We're taking you to a hospital. Don't worry.'

Jackson nods, glances towards the front seat, and who on earth is that? A woman has joined them but they only have this two-seater with a dickie seat and a two-stroke engine, useful for these small streets in Brunei, but there's hardly enough room for them to get all the way to the palace. The woman looks like Mrs Dominguez in Panama, who rented rooms to the workers from the dam and used to steal money from the pockets of the trousers they left in their rooms.

TWENTY-FIVE

Reema needs to do as Yosh says and calm her mind. She must write down what has happened, because she will have to report it to Jackson's family — but who is his family? She needs to remember the entire order of events, because she will be asked and she will be held accountable. She sits beside Yosh in the hospital waiting room, going over it all in her mind.

When they'd pulled over in the outskirts of Palampur, Yosh had got out and asked a shopkeeper for directions to the hospital. Which hospital, the man responded: Military Hospital? Civic Hospital? Children's Hospital? Leprosy Hospital? Yosh explained the situation and the man recommended the Vijay Choudhary Clinic, in the bazaar, near the Income Tax Office. But he did not warn them about the one-way street system in the centre of the town.

When they reached the roundabout, all traffic was diverted left, away from the fastest route to the clinic. Yosh turned right, into a one-way street whose oncoming traffic stopped them dead. Then it became a blur. The men, the motorcycle, the tiffin man, the small boy holding up his schoolbook. She needs to piece it all together.

She and Yosh are in the waiting area of the Palampur Civic Hospital, not the Vijay Choudhary Clinic, because one-way systems have their own destiny. The paint on the walls is fresh, the signs modern and in two languages. The hospital is at the end of the main road, on the north side of the bazaar. When the clinic proved impossible to reach, Yosh had got directions to the Civic Hospital from a man selling transistor radios. Even still, the one-way system wouldn't allow the jeep to merge with the road from the top of the roundabout, where they were faced with more approaching cars, scooters, trucks and autorickshaws. And there was no way to back up into the flow of vehicles.

'Where is it? Where?' Reema had shouted from the back seat, where Jackson was now lying with his head on her lap.

'At the end of this road, down there,' the radio seller called, and pointed in the direction of the oncoming cars.

Monica opened her door, got out and ran in the direction he was pointing, and only now does Reema understand her intention. She stopped a young man on his motorcycle and spoke to him. A moment later three men had lifted Jackson out of the jeep and were helping him onto the bike. Then they began to push the motorcycle down the road, dodging vehicles, Jackson half sitting, half lying, held in place by the men. Families made way for them and a tiffin shop owner followed along beside them, cooling Jackson's forehead with water from a bottle. A young boy shaded Jackson with his schoolbook. Other people followed the small entourage down the road towards the hospital the way they did visiting government ministers or film stars.

The hospital is cool and smells clean. She deliberately relaxes her shoulders.

'There,' Yosh says. 'Now: deep breaths.'

'Where is Monica?' she asks.

'Somewhere in town.'

'I should find her,' she says, and starts to stand. Monica had rushed to save him.

He takes hold of her arm gently to stop her. He mutters something so quietly she doesn't understand, but it has the cadence of a prayer.

'Rest a moment. She's okay. She needed some air.' His hand remains on her wrist, and she doesn't move it away. When he finally lets go, he looks at her as though to apologise.

But it's she who should explain to him that she's fine, that she wants to be outside again in the traffic because her mind was vacant in those few minutes along the one-way street. The feeling like being inside the tabla beat, or being under the magnolia tree in Kilburn, or staring at the skin tag on Robert's thigh — everything dangerous enfolded into everything else. And perfect. As she watched strangers transporting a sick old man on a motorcycle to where he might be saved, she was not in her own body, she was in the body of every person on the street. She would like to be there again. She needs to thank Monica.

In music the silences are as important as the notes, but this is not what she experienced on the road. Silence is difference from absence. Silence has a purpose, whereas what she felt was purposeless and absolute. And fine.

A man, woman and their young son arrive in the waiting room. Their faces drawn, in crisis. Reema does not want to stay here and feel anything. She wants to be back in the street.

'Text me, please, if there is any more news,' she says to Yosh, and gets up quickly, so that he can't stop her. 'I'll be back soon,' she says and heads out of the hospital.

———

The street is not as busy as it was. She looks left, right, wondering which direction Monica went in. She can't imagine what there is to photograph here, and surely they've all seen enough for one day. Jackson draped over a man wearing a motorcycle helmet, his legs splayed and hanging, his ankles puffed up like balloons at the end of his shins. Reema wanders towards the bazaar. Maybe Monica is hungry and has gone searching for dinner.

Men stare at her as she walks down the bazaar alley, past cauldrons with boiling oil, frying pakoras, puri, and simmering pots of kadai paneer. To them she is a fair-skinned Indian woman in the wrong clothes, a westerner who can be gawked at, but she is not cowed. Monica would not be. Monica demanded the motorcyclist stop and attend to Jackson in the car, insisted the other men help. After they wheeled him down the road, she came to stand for a moment beside Reema, where a middle-aged woman, her sari bright orange and green, came to their side.

'Papa?' the woman had asked, pointing to Jackson.

'No, no, friend,' said Monica, who was now trembling. The woman told them in Hindi, and then in scraps of English, that the hospital was good, that it helped her old mother, who had been sick a few months earlier. The woman invited them to her home, to have food, to take a rest, offering to bring them to the hospital to see their friend after they had eaten.

'We need to go with them now,' Monica said, as Reema told the woman, 'No, no, thank you, that's really kind.' The woman did not seem insulted, merely puzzled that such an offer would not be taken up, and she waved them on.

Perhaps Monica has found the woman again, and is at her home, eating tandoori aloo parathas and khatta saag.

Reema spots an ATM, new, clean, rare. She has only pocket change. If she's going to buy a meal for them all she needs cash.

She inserts her Visa card, follows instructions, enters her PIN, and waits. The machine tells her it cannot process her request. She hits the face of the machine gently. It spits out her card. She leaves the small booth and heads farther down the road. She spots a sign for the State Bank of India. She enters the booth. Invalid transaction. She tries again with the same result, then heads out in the opposite direction. She stops at a stall selling mangoes, bananas, and guava fruit.

A man in a long brown kurta, his eyes wrinkled, his hair grey and his face moist and shining, waits for her order. She points at the bananas and holds up two fingers; raises one finger over the mangoes; and two over the guava fruit. The man looks confused. She uses her weak Hindi to describe what she'd like. The man is still confused and looks around for help.

A young man on a scooter stops beside them. He lifts his helmet just up above his ears, so he can hear.

'What do you want?' he asks Reema.

Embarrassed, Reema tells him in English. The young man translates for the old man then gets off his scooter to pack her fruit in folded newspaper, patting the old man's shoulder to say *let me do it*. He hands each newspaper sac to Reema as he finishes folding. She loads them into her knapsack and takes out her wallet.

The old man says ninety rupees, and she gives him a hundred. She thanks the young man, who pulls his helmet back down over his face, hops back on his scooter and speeds away up the road. Reema shakes her head when the fruit seller offers her the change, but he seems confused again, so she takes the ten-rupee note, but then gives it back to him. He squints at her and she's worried she has offended him. She nods and smiles. He shrugs, not having expected this last phase of the transaction. She walks on, up the hill, wondering if the man on the motorcycle was the same one who'd helped Jackson. How many more helpful motorcyclists are there in Palampur? Between bodies and machines, the animate and inanimate: *takada takada da da*.

A few hours ago, inside the town's bustle, Reema's fingers were in the shirtsleeve of the man who held Jackson's head, her toes in the little boy's schoolbook, her eyes in a nuthatch on a tree branch, her heart in the cow lying at the side of the road, her mind in Jackson's, which was tired and without thought. Her torso had disappeared. Nothing to choose.

TWENTY-SIX

The tube that goes from the plastic bag to a thick vein in Jackson's hand is filled with something called Lasix. On her return to the hospital, as she wiped the guava juice from the side of her mouth, the doctor had told her that Lasix would help to eliminate the fluid that has built up around Jackson's lungs due to the old man's congestive heart failure. Lasix, the doctor said, is a miracle for someone with this condition, and without it Jackson would eventually drown in his own fluids. Not a pleasant death. But she must not be worried — Jackson will be fine if they can clear his lungs now. Congestive heart failure can take years to kill a man.

Reema watched vigilantly as the nurses carefully prepared the IV. The Lasix was transmitted through a saline solution, which would drip into Jackson from the bag as soon as the nurse rolled the small plastic clamp upwards. Reema took note of when the magical drip began.

The doctor had also inserted a catheter into the tip of Jackson's penis and had pushed a tube up to his bladder to allow urine to flow into the plastic bag now hanging from the side of the hospital bed. At his age, the doctor said, it was not surprising that Jackson had an enlarged prostate. Reema could only nod her head, trying to keep track for the unknown relatives she would have to tell.

Jackson is now asleep in his bed; seven men in identical beds share the ward with him. She can't see them all — many have their curtains drawn — but the tangy smells of illness, the moans, sighs and coughs, surround her. One man shouts out in pain. Another talks to himself, possibly in prayer. The nurses have put a chair beside Jackson's bed for Reema. She told them she was sure that Jackson could pay for a private room, so they have gone to arrange one.

Reema had searched Jackson's pockets and found his wallet, cards, and driver's licence, but no passport. The hospital administrator needs his passport, so she will have to ask Yosh to fetch his suitcase from the jeep. For now, though, she is just here. Jackson stirs every so often to ask where he is, but even then he is far away. She must call her own relatives soon. The sun is descending, and her cousin will worry if she has not made it to the plantation before dark. Only for a short moment does she think about calling Robert, but no — nothing here seems related to him.

Jackson makes noises, reaching for the IV drip.

'No, don't …' She tries to soothe him. 'Leave that — it's helping you.'

Jackson opens his eyes and scowls at her; he pulls down the sheet and wrenches the hospital gown to one side to reveal his swollen intubated penis.

'Get me out of here,' he shouts. 'Out!' He breathes like a bull. 'Out!'

Reema gets up to straighten the gown and pull the sheet up from around his knees. 'It's okay, it's okay, we will get you out of here soon, but they need to drain the fluid from your chest, Jackson.

The doctors know what they are doing — you —'

'Get the hell away from me! The dam is closed and we are not allowing anyone else to enter. Get out!'

Jackson's face is contorted, showing her a rage she's never seen from him. She listens for a nurse, for a reaction from the other patients or their visitors, but no one stirs. The thin light of dusk haloes the room, silent now that his breath is calming.

At last a nurse pulls back the curtain and enters. She checks Jackson's drip and pulse. He swats her away, and when she speaks to him gently in Hindi, he swats again. 'Who are you? Leave me alone!'

'Jackson, the nurse is helping you,' Reema says from where she has backed up into the corner.

He struggles to sit up. 'I don't need anyone's help! I want to get back to my room at the guest house. You saw it. You saw it with your own eyes and now you're lying. I must report it.'

'I give him something,' the nurse says to Reema and goes to fetch it. Reema cannot budge from the corner. Jackson tries to get up but falls back weakly against the thin hospital sheet that covers the plastic mattress. He tries again and when he fails, he begins to tear the IV needle from his wrist. Reema shouts, 'No!' stepping forward. He looks at her with shock.

'What the hell?' he says.

'What are you doing?'

'I have to fill in the tax forms,' he says, as though she's the one being unreasonable.

She takes a deep breath, then tries to convey with the calm tone of her voice that all is okay, everything is being done — his tax forms, the guest room — everything is in place. Jackson frowns, not quite believing her. But, at last, persuaded by her certainty, he sinks back into the pillow, stares up at the strange white ceiling, his eyes seeming to track a gecko climbing across it.

The nurse returns with some pills in a small paper cup. 'Sometimes the old, they don't like the sun going down,' she says.

Reema turns towards the far window of the ward, where the remaining daylight streams into the room. Jackson's outburst has quieted the other patients, as though he has won some contest. He obediently takes his pills.

'I'll be back soon,' Reema says to him, patting one of his feet through the sheet. She looks at the nurse as though for permission, and then leaves the ward. In the corridor she turns left, then right, and follows the signs to the toilet. Inside a small cubicle she stands with her forehead pressed against the door, her eyes closed.

She brings her mind back to the crowd in the street, to the motorcycle that carried Jackson towards the hospital, but she can't feel it again. She tries to feel for the sound — *takada takada* — but she hears only the roar of motorcycles. As a girl in school she learned a trick of repeating a line of a song or an image in her mind over and over again, and somehow that would allow her to dream standing up, at sporting days, assemblies, even during long choir recitals. She would take herself away while appearing to be present. Time would stand still. She tries it now. Robert is with her on the sofa in her flat; they face each other, only inches apart, and he is playing with her hair. They speak softly of things she mentions to no one else: the way milk tastes different after the first sip; how irritating wind can be; the patterns of the damp stains on the ceiling that look like animals; the names of every shade of green that comes to mind. They giggle at nothing; they kiss. And it's that night that he comes so deeply inside her that she's sure something has changed. Still, even when they see that the condom has broken, she doesn't acknowledge her certainty to him.

She rubs her face with her hands and leaves the cubicle.

———

Yosh is still in the waiting room, with a few other people also patiently waiting. What she sees is not a man, a yoga teacher, an Indian or Canadian; she sees his animal form. His arms, shoulders, head alert, his eyes dart around the room until they rest on hers. A cougar or perhaps a gazelle. To this vision of him she is lost. He stares at her, not rising immediately.

She breaks her trance, to say 'We need to get his passport from the jeep. And to call Jyoti's father to contact the brother. Jackson must have insurance. I hope we'll find everything in his suitcase.' He nods and gets up to follow her.

'Monica sent a text while you were with him,' he says. 'She's rented a hotel room just at the edge of the market, and says they have room for us too.'

'Okay, but I have to arrange things for Jackson. There's a lot, I think. I don't know anything about what to do for him, but Jyoti will know.'

It's dark by the time they reach the jeep, in a paved car park several streets to the south of the hospital.

And then it must be the cougar or gazelle that takes over because suddenly they are embracing and her hips and shoulders are against the back of the jeep. His hand on her face. His mouth on hers. Her arms fly around his shoulders and hold on. He presses his pelvis to hers. She pulls him even closer. She feels the hardness there in his jeans. His tongue is wide and gentle. His hand moves from her face to her neck to her collarbone. She could split in two here. But at last she turns her head to the side, and gently pushes him away. His eyes are closed, and when he opens them, he reaches to smooth her shirt, pulling it down to cover the skin above her hips.

'I'm sorry,' he says.

She meets his eyes and shakes her head — no need to be sorry — then straightens up, touching her back where the metal pressed into her skin. Yosh lifts the suitcase out of the boot, extends the handle and offers it to her. She turns and pulls it back to the hospital, knowing that his eyes are on her every step, waiting for her to turn back, to change her mind and run towards him.

TWENTY-SEVEN

Jackson's private room has barely enough space for the fold-up camp bed that the nurse has kindly placed there. She shows Reema the hinge to unfold it when she is ready.

Jackson is asleep, still hooked to the IV, finally sedated. The pills took their time to produce the required effect. After she'd gone with Yosh to retrieve his bag, he had succeeded in tearing the catheter from his penis, blood and urine spraying the bed and the surrounding curtain, the traces of it still fresh when Reema got back.

Two young men, who were steady, sure and competent, and yet could not have been more than teenagers, moved him here. When they left her alone with Jackson she wanted to call for them to come back, to keep her company and to tell her how she was going to manage if he woke up again and began to shout and pull at his tubes. But he seems peaceful now. The skin on his face is nearly translucent, with brown spots like gigantic freckles, its dry scaly surface giving way to something soft around his eyes. She has never stared so closely at such an old person for so long. There is that spike of white hair protruding from the mole behind his ear, which she noticed that first day at the wedding. She shifts her eyes from his face to his hand, and then to the palm of her own. She turns it over. The creases of her knuckle, are smooth lines, not the crevices of Jackson's hand. Skin grows, stretches, does not retract. Skin is impossible to understand.

She turns to his suitcase and lifts it up onto the folding bed. It's remarkably light. She unzips the main compartment. So little inside: a few boxer shorts, toiletries, an undershirt, a shirt and the tea canister, which she picks up, finding it heavier than she'd expected. She places it back carefully between the folded clothes and toiletries. She's seen him wearing other clothes and wonders if he's forgotten them at the Pink House. His passport is hidden in an inner compartment. She opens it to look at the more youthful photograph, the dates of issue and expiration, and, yes, there, written in the back, the next of kin: Amelia. Only Amelia.

Inside Jackson there are tiny cracks opening between the light and dark — green and orange flashes. The cracks are joining up, growing. He tries to open his eyes, but there is a weight like a hand over them. The hand has sand wedged into the lines of its palm. The sand makes gritty spots on his thoughts.

——

When Reema returns to Jackson's room she feels more confident that she has things under control. Jyoti's father knows Jackson's brother, who is even older than Jackson, but Jyoti has assured her that her father will notify the niece and nephew, and she's not to worry. The one who lives in Dubai will contact the one who lives in Sydney, and they will decide what is right; their uncle is their father's only brother, and their uncle is alone in the world. With Indian families this aloneness is unusual, but Reema knows that many old men like Jackson have only neighbours and friends to support them. Jyoti is certain that the niece and nephew will do what is right, immediately;

Reema is grateful and relieved. She stands over Jackson and takes hold of his misshapen arthritic index finger. He is in the same position she left him in, which feels eerie.

'You are a lucky man,' she whispers. 'All these people making a fuss about you.'

She turns to the cot and unhooks the hinge so that it springs out to its full length. It is too big and blocks the door. She folds it up and sits on the floor, her eyes heavy, leaning her head on the steel frame of the cot. Her neck soon becomes stiff. She stands up and releases the cot again. She'll lie down just for a few minutes.

TWENTY-EIGHT

It's hot. The mandibles of an insect move side to side rather than up and down. Young people walk out of their offices, carrying the contents of their desks in small boxes. The television is not plugged in. Lehman Brothers, lemur, oh brother, not langur. The astrologist in Delhi had only one eye. The tubes. The oxygen. Jackson is awake. The Bhakra Dam is delayed and he must take some of the blame. Jackson is asleep. His father was very grateful to the Venezuelan veterinarian for looking after Jackson while he was at the rig. Oh look, the tiny jewels at the horse's ankle make the sun blue.

Jackson is awake. There are langurs on the ceiling. Someone is standing beside him in the alley and he has seen something that Jackson hasn't. He leaves, quickly, but he too does not call out. Jackson is asleep. There are no snakes in Boston. Geysers of oil in 1929, Dad, what did you expect? No two women can sing alike. But a dam is not a geyser. The men in kurta pyjamas circle the woman in the headscarf. Look, Jackson, there on the cross-country ski trail in the Noanet Woodlands, your wife's ass. No, not there, here, in Amritsar. Jackson is young. Drinking with the men in the kurta pyjamas who worked on the dam project. Insect mandibles can dig, fight, cut, collect food. The wishing tree, the wedding garden, the branches weighed down with wishes for children. He stumbled back to Mrs Bhandari's guest house.

One of the dam engineers had a sprained wrist, wrapped in cloth and tape. Concrete dams are stronger than earth-filled dams. He bragged of his bulky physique. But the Bengali engineer was a Hindu. Why did he have such a big watch? He was educated in England, the accountant said. The Punjabi man said that since Gandhi had been shot they were free to avenge. English gin in bottle after bottle. There was no yoga teacher, no one to tame them all, and what? Such long hair. What did he say? What did the man with the Rolex say? Drawn the short stick. In Brunei the sun sets at the same time all year long. In Venezuela the Carora cattle were selectively bred for the finest milk. Jackson, wake up. The schooner will be sunk by the Germans. Boston winter afternoons are typhoons of sex one year when he expects it least. But Gandhi's murderer is not a Muslim, said the man with the sprained wrist. Drawn the short stick. The other man's voice sank when he said, in any case I drew the trump, because by the time it was my turn she was dead and I carried a heap of cold flesh and then what good was she? Jackson, wake up. The other man was an accountant. But that didn't stop me trying, the other man said. Both laughing. The same accountant who showed Jackson the photo of the fleeing men, arms like wings. The same accountant who told him how long it takes to drown a circumcised teenage boy as timed by the engineer's expensive watch. Jackson is asleep. *Guldasta*, drive faster, the clothes need stitching. The next day at the dam office there is a sprained wrist, a Rolex watch. He knows what he did not know, but still he does not report it. They killed the woman while they tried to fuck her. From this vantage point in the alley you can see some things but not all, but you can know what you cannot see. And, oh, Jackson, wake up.

So what will you say to Reema? What can be said? The banks failed. What will you tell the young people? That the water from the dam is released slowly. It is. People are warned. They are. No one knew there were still people in the valley. Look, a cuckoo. In Bengali its call is 'Bride, please speak'... and on and on it cries. The woman with the missing arm: all she wanted to do was give them a child. Come on, buddy. The langurs are on the ceiling. Reema, listen. He's sorry. He didn't see. No, he did see. He didn't know what he saw. A woman? He didn't say. A piece of straw? That's it. He didn't say. The next day he performed his job, did as he was told. Cowards are the most evil of all. He should have danced with Amelia on New Year's Eve. A coward doesn't dance. He has looked away. He has looked the other way. He might as well have been the one who had drowned them all.

TWENTY-NINE

'Reema! Reema!'

She is startled awake and sits up so fast she pulls something in her neck. The night outside the window is still black, the only light coming in under the bottom of the door.

'Reema!' Jackson is sitting up, his sheets thrown off, nearly out of bed.

As she approaches he throws his arms around her and she stumbles back but manages to take his weight and hold him steady.

'I tried to get to you,' Jackson cries, 'but they were laughing, but you're safe, you have nothing to worry about, Yosh won't hurt you, I've killed him, I've killed the whole lot of them. It's finally done.'

She pushes him gently down on the bed. He is ghost-pale in the darkness. His eyes roll in delirium.

'Jackson,' she says, softly, and lets him fall towards her again. She holds his head against her shoulder. 'It's okay. Everything is okay. I'm here.'

He is breathing in rapid gasps, which give way to smoother, longer breaths, until eventually he is calm. His arms drop from around her and she guides him towards the pillow.

He stares up at her, as though making sure it's really her, taking her in.

'I'm here,' she says. She takes his hand and he nods.

She hears noises at the end of the corridor, the sound of beeping and machine hums, someone talking quietly. She rubs his hand in the darkness.

Soon she thinks he has fallen back to sleep, but as she moves to go back to her cot, he raises his head. She rubs his hand again.

'Where's my mother?' he asks in a whisper.

'She's passed,' she says, as gently as she can.

'Ah?' He shakes his head.

The voices have quietened.

'Where is my father?'

'He's passed as well.'

'Oh.'

'And my wife?'

'She's passed, too, Jackson, remember? Amelia.'

His forehead creases. He shakes his head as if to deny it, but then, with clear and calm certainty, he says, 'I shouldn't have let them go before me.'

She smooths his forehead. She wants to tell him that he's not going, that the Lasix is helping him, but he seems so calm now, she says nothing. He closes his eyes and falls back to sleep.

She watches his face for signs that he is truly peaceful again. But in it there is another sign, like an indecipherable pattern in dust. She returns to the cot and lies down.

———

This time a pounding at the door wakes her. She sits up. The cot is blocking the door; she hears panicked voices in the corridor.

'Just a minute!' she calls, glancing at Jackson, who is staring up at the ceiling. She folds up the cot as quickly as she can and opens the door for the nurse, who chastises her in Hindi. 'I fell asleep, I'm sorry,' she says. The nurse changes the IV bag, adds more medication, then leaves. It's almost dawn, she realises, but the sky is not yet light. Silence returns and Reema sits in the chair beside the bed, tuning in to Jackson's breathing as he continues to stare at the ceiling. She hears less of a gurgle; the Lasix is working. She stands up and walks to the end of the bed. She touches his feet, too timid to lift the sheet to look at his ankles, but she imagines that they are normal, not swollen any more.

'How are you feeling?'

Has he heard her? She moves to his side. Jackson looks her in the eye and for a moment she's frightened again. 'Are you feeling better?' He continues to stare at her, his face blank. She touches his arm, noticing that the IV drip seems to have stopped. Panicking, she goes out into the corridor to find help. The nurse's station is abandoned, and no one seems to be moving about the floor. She returns to Jackson's room, certain she knows what she has to do. She takes hold of the IV's roller clamp, just as the nurse had done, and moves the plastic lever up. The drip starts, but too fast. She panics and closes it again.

She leans over, trying to make eye contact, but Jackson is staring somewhere else. 'I will call Jyoti again,' she says. 'She's probably heard from your family …' She hesitates. 'I'll go and find out when they'll get here, and then come back.' He makes no sound. 'Okay,' she says. She pats his foot again and leaves the room.

Of course Yosh isn't in the waiting room this time, but she's still disappointed. She had imagined him returning here, to spend the night on a chair to be near to her. Her throat is dry with Palampur dust, and she has slept for too many hours in the smell of Jackson's decay. She needs his help.

She leaves the hospital. A few people are awake, going about the opening of their shops and stalls; there are very few vehicles on the streets, and some sleeping cows. She realises she doesn't know the name of the hotel where Monica and Yosh are staying. She turns in one direction, takes a few steps, sees only a man sweeping the pavement with a leafy branch. A few cars with their headlights on approach up the hill. She turns back the other way and walks around the main roundabout of the town, twice.

The sky seems slow to brighten. She decides to head down the road parallel to the main street. Her neck is stiff, but at least she doesn't feel nausea this morning. She takes out her phone to text Jyoti. What if Jackson's family doesn't come to get him? Will she have to be the one to stay, to fly with him to Delhi from Gaggal, get him on a plane to Boston and hope that he has someone to meet him there? Where do we go when we are old and alone? Her own parents are still young; they live among friends and family, between London, Delhi, San Francisco. Her parents do not need her.

She sees a text she has missed, from Yosh.

'Hotel near Ram Market called Mountain View. Look for red sign next to ATM.'

She has no idea where that is. She texts Jyoti: 'Help.' She puts the phone in her bag and walks towards the street sweeper. 'Ram Market?' she says. He tells her in elaborate detail how to find it. She walks in the general direction he is pointing.

The Mountain View Hotel has no particular view except of

small buildings, chai shops, a bank and the Ram Market. Perhaps there are rooms on the third floor above the buildings from which you can see snow-capped peaks.

She enters the lobby of the hotel and smells mildew. She clears her throat. At reception, she speaks to a man with round spectacles and asks if she can sit and wait for her friends. Of course, he says, nodding in the direction of two tattered armchairs at the edges of a tribal rug.

She texts Monica. Then she taps a message to her cousin at the tea plantation to tell her that if things go as planned she'll arrive later today.

'Hey,' Monica says, and Reema looks up. She is so relieved to see her that she stands up and hugs her, dropping the phone on the rug.

'How is he?' Monica says, hugging her back.

'He's going to be fine. They are taking care of him,' Reema says. 'How are you?'

'Tired,' she says. 'Not much sleep — music and noise all night. Also, I wanted to tell you that I need to leave. Yosh can decide what he wants to do, but I've got to go now. There are things I need to do.'

Reema feels suddenly lonely. 'Of course, of course. I'm going too, to my family, as soon as I know Jackson is taken care of. My flight home is in two days.'

Reema hears someone on the stairs and turns to see Yosh, who slows at the sight of her. There is still the trace of animal forms between them. She walks towards him.

'He's doing much better,' Reema says.

He smiles at both of them as though it is their success, the three of them.

'I will talk to the doctors. We can then make plans?' he says. He looks at Monica and then at Reema, but the idea of a plan, of leaving this town, of not being on the road walking behind the motorcycle, is nearly impossible for Reema to imagine.

———

Three abreast, they walk to the hospital.

On Jackson's floor, Reema says, 'You go ahead, I'll be right there,' and points to the door of the toilet she needs to use.

When she comes out, she sees Monica walking swiftly away from her down the corridor.

Reema enters Jackson's room. The nurse who is bent over Jackson has a sweat streak down her spine in the shape of a palm tree. Another nurse folds up a cord, winding it between her forefinger and thumb and down around her elbow. The machine that the cord is attached to is dark, silent. And it's the movement of the cord being wrapped up and down, up and down, the length of the woman's forearm, that Reema gets stuck on. She can't make out what on earth the nurse is doing with all that cord.

Yosh is standing beside the bed with his eyes closed. She feels as though the floor before her is wide and porous. Yosh opens his eyes. She waits for him to say something, but he is silent.

She frowns as the nurses roll the IV stand away. Reema looks at the bed.

Jackson's mouth is open, his hands by his side, where the nurses have placed them.

She moves closer and lifts the sheet to examine his feet. His ankles are less swollen, she thinks. She lets the sheet fall over his feet again. Her throat tightens.

She turns to Yosh and her face says, *What on earth?*

'He was never going to make it,' Yosh says.

This can't be true. *I'll come back,* she'd said to him. She was always coming back. She surveys the room, noticing only now that the walls are yellow. The green ceiling is low. Out the window, the bough of a huge tree. The cot on which she spent the night has been removed. She moves towards the top of the bed and leans over Jackson, trying to make sure that what she's seeing is really true. His eyes are closed, his cheekbones pronounced. The dried scab of blood across his eyebrow is darker, looks nearly artificial against his dusty skin. He doesn't look like himself. His face doesn't look like anyone she has ever known. *Don't jump, fishy.* She touches his forehead as she has been doing these last few days. There is still warmth there; the skin is soft. 'I'm back,' she says, and begins to cry.

———

The sounds in the corridor of the hospital are muted. No one is calling out; machines are clinking, beeping. The white noise is like a waterfall. Yosh has his arm around Monica, who is crying.

'Someone has to sign the papers,' Yosh says. 'We must leave this to his family, I think.'

'It's terrible,' Monica quavers.

Reema shakes her head in disbelief, again and again. What has happened? There's a family story of seeing a dead person when she was a baby. It's deep in her imagination like her own memory. As her brother tells it, she's sitting on his lap in the back seat of their car in Delhi, when he gasps and she starts. She follows her brother's finger, which points out to the road: the man lies on his side, his shirt unbuttoned and ribs exposed, his trousers in tatters below the knee. His face is planted on the pavement at an impossible angle. He has one slipper on, the other having been flung somewhere far, far from death, still belonging to the man, but now lost. The traffic moves past him and the image is gone. Throughout their childhood, her brother teased her that her looking at the man was what had killed him. She'd stared at Jackson lying on the bed as though she had been flung far away, like the dead man's shoe.

She wants to comfort Monica, to tell her that what happened in that room — with the palm tree sweat mark, the folding and folding of the dark machine's cord, and the smell of something having been singed — might be exactly what they have all been meant to witness. For Monica, maybe it wasn't Shimla, the Dalai Lama, or Buddha she came to India for, while her banking colleagues were numbing themselves with sedatives. No, it has been this ordinary fact in this ordinary town on this ordinary day — that a man has died even after they have tried to save him.

THIRTY

They walk up the main road in Palampur towards the roundabout, and she feels Yosh reining himself in — not reaching out to take her hand or put his arm around her shoulder the way he had with Monica. Perhaps he is imagining, as she is, him lifting her up in his arms, to kiss her, to taste her wet face. Monica has retreated to the hotel he has found them, much more comfortable than the Mountain View. She is waiting for them there.

'There's nothing for us to do until his nephew gets here,' Yosh is saying. 'The hospital will keep his body in the morgue, because he's a foreigner. Normally Hindus would cremate within twenty-four hours, but there is a law, even for foreigners. If they don't want him cremated within the week, they must come now … and the nephew must register the death. He must come immediately.'

'He will. From Dubai,' she says. Look, she is being practical. She can't bring herself to tell Yosh about touching the roller clamp of the IV drip, that small piece of plastic, that mechanism. She can feel it in her fingers. 'But I don't think they were close — how will he know what Jackson would want? Jackson didn't even know this for his wife.' She stops suddenly.

'What?'

'Amelia,' she says. They must go back to get her. He immediately understands, and nods, but checks his watch.

'Let's take a moment to talk about what we should do,' Yosh says, and looks for somewhere they can sit. On the side of the road is a café with an ice-cream freezer out front. The sign says Joy Café. This can't be right. This doesn't seem right, but that is where he leads her.

He points up at the sign. 'Jackson would have had a laugh, yes?'

'Yes,' she says, but nothing is funny. Inside the restaurant the air is cool and the decor of dark wrought-iron tables and chairs is sombre enough. She looks up at the menu board. Milkshakes and ice cream, paneer masala, hot dogs, dosas.

Yosh orders chai; they push away the menus and lay their hands on the table. His fingers tear small pieces from a paper napkin. Her hands remain still.

Reema says, 'What about Amelia?' She must see this through. Where is the damn snow?

'If she was Indian, she would be scattered in water, not on land,' he says, his face so serious, 'and it would have been done directly after the cremation.'

'Yes.' Clear or muddy water? A riverbank or a reservoir? Water to submerge a whole village in.

What do you do after a death? She knows nothing. When her grandmother died, her mother went to Kangra for the cremation alone while her father stayed in London to look after Reema and her brother. 'Jackson wanted snow,' Reema says. 'There is snow high up in the passes.'

'I could go up,' Yosh offers. 'I have five more days before I need to get to Delhi for my flight.'

She pinches her finger and thumb together, considers the trick of the repeated song so that she might detach from all of this. It's her fault, is it not? She must be the one to go. At the snow line, Jackson will meet Amelia. But Reema has run out of time. This valley. Her body. The moment is passing.

'I think Jackson would have preferred the Gangotri Glacier, the source of the Ganges,' Yosh is saying, and she looks up from where she is, at the edge of this conversation. Their chai has arrived. 'It would be the place to scatter her ashes. Hindus believe that if a person dies in the Ganges or has Ganges water sprinkled on them at the end, it means that they will achieve absolute salvation, and will not have to repeat the cycle of reincarnation. But it's far from here.'

Reema doesn't say anything. Water, like lymph, like tea.

Yosh goes on. 'He is not a Hindu. I never understood why he brought her all the way here.'

'I don't know why.'

She wants to tell him about her conversation with Jackson on the mountain, when he told her that he was a man who had loved only one woman, and how a man can love a woman and still not know what is right for her. She wants to lean across the table, pushing his chai to the side, to tell him all these things. Don't burn, don't drown. Come this way.

'You've been to cremations here?' she says.

He nods. 'The first was my great-uncle's, when I was young. We travelled from Delhi back to my parents' village in Maharashtra. We didn't make it in time to see the ceremony. My father's cousin was very angry at him, saying that since the rich brother-in-law had forgotten his family, they went ahead without us. We arrived to embers, and I was so disappointed.' He looks up at her and smiles. 'I was a boy. I was sad I didn't get to see the skull explode and the soul released to heaven.'

She sits back and breathes in as deep as she can, as if through smoke, looking down at her hands. She is exhausted by everything.

'I wanted to ask my uncle if the skull had cracked open by itself or if he had to help the release, but I was too shy,' he says. 'I was a good Hindu boy.'

Reema's father is a Christian who once tried to be a Hindu; her mother used to be a Hindu and just wants to be modern. She and her brother were expected to be good children, good immigrants, good brown people. She's been a problem on all scores — for her parents, and for Yosh, for Monica, for everyone who must now act on behalf of two dead strangers.

Yosh has said something, and she waits for him to repeat it.

'You could come with me to the river.'

She looks up. She scans for the cougar.

The jeep would go higher, where clouds rest. And music. And snow. Animals watching from the top of crevices, birds singing. She would sing.

But there is no cougar. The angles of his face are sharp and human. He is outside of anything that is possible at the moment.

Jackson would have made purposeful footsteps in the snow. For love. But she is like Monica's auntie's ghost, facing the other way. Is she walking towards or away? Her feet are turned backwards.

'I like you,' she says. She feels his reaction. She feels hers. 'But you don't even know me.'

After a time, he nods. Of all the motions of the body available to them, this is most apt. There is a lie in what she has said. He does know her, perhaps better than anyone in her life in London, knowing from his own forwards and backwards that freedom might not be the issue.

'Maybe we should write to each other,' he says at last, 'the old-fashioned way, with pen and paper.'

The ghost with feet turned backwards cries in the night. What she wants is for him to hold her against the wall of this café and refuse to let her go back to London.

'I don't know,' she says. 'Maybe.'

They sip their chai.

He concentrates on his cup. She wonders whether he is focusing on pranayama the way he teaches it. Finding the front wall of his lungs, filling them with new air, right to the top, under his collarbone. He taught her to pause at the top, and in the exhale to find the back wall of the lungs.

Reema would like to have a master, as he had. She would like someone to teach her how to make the ordinary extraordinary, to distract her body from its own surprises, to walk on the edges of her feet to find balance, to turn around, to face any which way.

THIRTY-ONE

The dead calf in the meadow at Pong Dam had been eaten clean by vultures; its horns, bones and hide left like a perfect maquette of a cow. On the meadow everything was still. She was learning to be Indian, squatting, singing the bull and the peacock, flying in the V of cormorants, feeling safe even in a flooded valley. But nothing is safe or as forward as it seems.

Reema arrives at the nurse's station, preparing to confront the woman who changed the IV bag, wanting to know if the roller clamp should have been closed for those moments while Reema was gone. The nurse stares at her, waiting for Reema to speak.

'I need his suitcase,' Reema says softly. 'Please.'

The nurse leads her to the locker where the suitcase has been stored. Reema lifts it out and lays it flat on the floor. She takes out the tea canister. Around her the hospital is once again busy and noisy. She closes the suitcase, returns it to the locker, and picks up the canister.

She leaves the hospital with Amelia gently resting in her hands. She walks slowly, with respect. She once held her paternal grandmother's ashes in a heavy urn that had been sent from California. Her father buried it in their garden in north London under a now-stunted salai tree, which he had hoped would one day bear frankincense that he would use to treat his stiff ankle. But the tree has never flowered, and her father has a permanent limp. Jackson would appreciate this story.

When she gets to the other side of the one-way system, she walks towards the car park near the fruit stand she'd awkwardly patronised. The old fruit seller is nowhere in sight. A young boy in western dress lays out rows of hessian sacks along the road beside the stall. Reema crosses the street and spots the jeep in the shade of the only tree in the car park. Yosh and Monica are already seated inside.

She pauses. If she went with them, would Monica be her friend? Would Yosh be her lover? They could have days unlike any of their parents could ever have imagined for them.

London is quiet inside her — cold, damp, and irrelevant. She listens. Her body tells her nothing. The time limit for mifepristone and misoprostol is ten weeks. Nearly there. Robert has gone completely silent, and she has not reached out to him.

Monica and Yosh step out of the jeep as she comes nearer, Yosh moving towards her like a dancer approaching a lift. For a brief moment she is thrilled, and Monica looks away as though she's intruding on this dance. But then he slows down.

'Well, here it is,' Reema says. She hands him the canister. Yosh nods, formally.

'I'll take care of her,' he says. 'Monica has agreed to come with me.'

Monica nods. All these nods and affirmations among them. But Reema's feet are facing backwards. She will wait at the Joy Café for her cousin to pick her up, as they'd arranged. She closes her eyes briefly and nods her gratitude to them both.

Yosh carries the canister to the jeep and slides it into a small nylon pouch that he takes from the boot. Finding a secure place between suitcases, he wedges the pouch in there. 'We'll go to a pass I know where there is still snow. It will be a hike, but we have the time.'

The car park is surprisingly empty. This is not a day for shoppers or for business, and there are only a few other cars stationed here. The heat is intense, no breeze, and the tree is thin, casting scant, uneven shade.

'Have a nice time with your family,' Monica says. Before Reema can say anything in return, Monica pulls her into a hug.

'I'm so glad we met,' Reema says into Monica's shoulder.

Monica lets go, and steps back, smiling. 'Yeah. Look me up if you come to Toronto.'

There could be a life in which this is possible. 'I will,' she says.

She turns to Yosh to see if there will be the lift after all, but he is climbing into the driver's seat. Monica heads around the car and opens her door.

Reema hears Yosh say, 'I will get petrol and then we can be off.' Monica seems as surprised as Reema that this is how things will end between the two.

When Yosh puts the jeep into gear, Reema waves, like a girl whose family is leaving her behind for the summer. Monica and Yosh wave back. The jeep moves slowly past a few parked cars. Reema counts silently from ten backwards, holding on to her smile, showing nothing else on her face. The brake lights brighten as the jeep stops at the exit, then turns right onto the main road.

THIRTY-TWO

Amritsar is different. It's not Pathankot, Dharmsala, or Palampur — not in architecture, or hills or views of snow. It doesn't have the diffuse light of polluted Delhi. Amritsar light is sharp and demanding.

It's not just the difference in dress, the sudden appearance of brightly coloured turbans on young men in western clothing, and on older men in stark white kurta pyjamas, or the differently patterned chunni or shape of the shoes on some women. The streets of Amritsar are as crowded, rubbish-lined, bicycle-filled, motorcycle-humming as anywhere else she's been on this trip, but there is something different here that she can't yet pinpoint.

Her cousin's private driver took her the three hours from the tea plantation in Palampur to the five-star hotel in the centre of Amritsar, where she'd booked Reema a hotel room. Reema took one look, and knew it was a place she couldn't stay. She has another place in mind, if she can find it. Now she is in an autorickshaw, which is taking her to the Golden Temple.

They come to a stop in the heavily congested street that leads towards the temple. A cyclist in a striped cotton vest pulls up beside her. He looks at her with interest, but at the sight of an opening between cars he pedals his bicycle through it and turns off to the right. Persistent honking neutralises her thoughts. She concentrates on the hooves of the cow at the side of the road, the hair of the woman with the sheer pink chunni draped over her head and falling over her shoulder.

The difference in Amritsar, she realises at last, is the absence of Yosh. She thinks of texting him to say she's arrived in Amritsar and will take an early flight to Delhi, then back to London, after a stay in Mrs Bhandari's guest house. She would like him to stay with her there. But she keeps her phone in her pocket.

'You must see the Golden Temple,' Jackson had said to her at Masroor with blood dripping onto his cheek from his forehead. He'd said it as though he meant, *don't take it out on the temples after this, see them all*. 'And stay at Mrs Bhandari's,' he'd added, and described for her the refugees during Partition, the chaos, people not understanding which side would keep them safe.

For her Amritsar is more significant for earlier events — a city under the gun of British generals, soldiers opening fire to slaughter innocent people gathered at a festival. When she had learned about it in school, she had felt both devastated by and responsible for the massacre, as though her English great-grandfather himself had gunned down her Indian great-grandfather. There was never any way that this could be reconciled inside her.

Her cousin's tea plantation covered the slope of a valley, with rows of tea shrubs growing below the house, which had a view of a mountain range across the valley. The plantation was busy with workers, but also with Indian tourists, who had rented the bungalows further down the slope and who dined at the main house morning and night — a home that would not have looked out of place in Europe, a luxurious space maintained by servants. Her cousin had plans for her — a tour of the plantation, dinner the next night with friends and relatives — but Reema had quickly found herself using the story of the last few days as an excuse. 'I can only stay with you tonight. Jackson wanted me to go to the temple in Amritsar.' To pray, she thought, but didn't say. To pray so that she might understand what had just happened.

The autorickshaw skids to an abrupt halt near the main gates to the Golden Temple. The driver apologises over and over again for the skid. A man selling newspapers calls out. On his shoulder a parrot perches peacefully. Another man selling sweets waves and waves for the autorickshaw to keep moving, so it won't block traffic. A man cut in front of him, the driver tells Reema. Misunderstanding, she thinks he adds, the man is a flower.

Amritsar is dry, flat, no surrounding hills, the snow hundreds of miles away. And everything in this city leads to this spot upon which she has just arrived. Now she feels the absence of Jackson as well as Yosh, nervous about being on her own in the city. Come, monkey. She is struck with sudden, aching regret that she is not high in a mountain pass with Amelia and the others. But these backwards feet need to straighten out.

Looking at the crowds gathering at the temple gates, she closes her eyes again to try to dissolve into the hands and legs and ears of other people, the eyes of the parrot. The feeling doesn't come.

She follows the signs and instructions. At a large counter she gives her shoes and backpack to a man in a green turban. The man hands her a ticket and places her shoes in one of the hundreds of cubbyholes in the repository, her backpack in another. The turbans of the other shoe-keepers are all different colours: bright blue, purple, black, saffron, pink. Colourful men in the service of shoes. She feels certain that she will never see her belongings again. But never mind, her feet are tough, and the thought of her shoes being left here gives her a tiny thrill as she approaches the main entrance.

She feels the chanting in the air in her own throat. The singing is coming from behind the gates of the temple, past the threshold of the water where she must stop to wash her feet. She dips one foot and then the other. There is a sign that tells her that her head must be covered before she enters the temple. A man in a white turban points to a basket of scarves. She sifts through them and chooses a small blue and white cotton kerchief already tied to make a bandana. She adjusts it on her head. The vibration of the chanting travels through her chest. She hears more singers, and stringed instruments, from deeper inside the temple grounds. She scratches her head under the kerchief and tries not to dwell on the other heads this kerchief has covered. The chanting that goes on day and night here has an energy that draws her forward. She scratches her head again. She focuses on her feet as she enters the grounds. A world appears.

The Golden Temple is at the centre of a shallow holy lake, like a palace with a moat. The structure itself is smaller than she had imagined. Surrounding the Harmandir Sahib are white marble buildings forming a square city on water. The sounds come from all directions. The chanting, the stringed instruments and drums, the sound of people. Sadhana has given her an introduction to this music: the Gurbani Kirtan are hymns for love, for marriage, for children, for funerals, for hard times.

She walks to the right, around the perimeter of the holy lake, peering inside the marble buildings to find out what happens in them. Her opinionated cousin told her it was wise to visit the Golden Temple — the nectar of immortality — and that she would not regret it. While her cousin talked, Reema had examined her face; she was convinced that she had used products that had lightened her skin and had had plastic surgery on her neck. All evening, as her cousin had gone on and on about what kind of man she should marry, Reema tried to reply in her childish Hindi. But her cousin refused, telling her she sounded like a baby, and that, besides, it was much better to speak in English. English was their language, the language of tea.

On the edge of the holy lake there are families gathered, taking photos of one another. Young women, men, small children, older women, old men being helped by younger ones: her cousin had said that in Sikhism there is no need for a welfare state — for children's homes or old people's homes. Even if you are a Muslim, Jew, Sufi, Hindu, Christian, or Buddhist, you will be looked after if you are in need.

There are four entrances to the temple, many angles with which to approach your need. She walks towards a family consisting of a man, woman, grandmother and four children ranging from a toddler to teenagers. They sit on the marble ledge at the edge of the lake and seem to be listening as one to the Gurbani coming from loudspeakers behind them. Suddenly the littlest child, who could be no more than three — her dress frilled and lacy, a bright red that stands out against the white marble — stands up and begins to dance. She spins and spins, her small legs working to keep her turning. Reema would like to sit beside them. Not to have them look after her or talk to her. Just to sit there, like that, inside the hymn with them. The young girl grabs the hem of her dress, holds it out, and keeps spinning as her family smiles at her.

Reema moves on along the marble perimeter, wishing she could decipher the Sanskrit written on the walls. She joins the long queue to the Langar Hall. As she gets closer, she smells the food being shared here and sees people taking metal plates from a pile. They stand and wait for the karah prasad, each visitor taking prasad and then offering a small bow before moving along to collect dahl, chapatti, vegetables. Women sit together on the floor of the dining area, some using their hands to eat, some using forks. Reema turns around and leaves the queue, heading back to the marble path around the holy lake. She wants to do as her cousin instructed her, to understand the hospitality in the Langar Hall which feeds fifty thousand people a day, but she isn't ready for all of that yet.

She leaves the temple, tossing the headscarf into the basket from which she took it and fetching her shoes and backpack, handed over to her by a different man, this one young, his turban saffron-coloured and worn small and tight to his head.

She walks out into the open square. She needs rupees to pay for an autorickshaw to Mrs Bhandari's guest house and for her room, so at the ATM a little farther down the square she takes out the maximum amount. As she walks back towards the temple, the chanting can be heard from beyond the temple wall.

Two young men — no, teenagers, one only about fourteen years old — approach her, chatting to each other. When they are close the younger one grabs her right breast and squeezes it, so quickly that no one else notices, but violently enough to make Reema gasp. The boys keep walking, chattering away. Her rage takes hold, and she turns to go after them but the only words that come are

AH FUCK! People see and hear only this — a crazed uncovered woman swearing at the top of her lungs. *Ah fuck.* Then, to herself, *You fucking idiot.* She stamps her foot and turns back to where the rickshaws are parked.

———

A turquoise-painted iron gate clearly marks her destination: Mrs T. Bhandari, 10 Cantonment.

She rings the bell. Nothing stirs on the other side. She rings it again and waits. Knocking would be wiser, she thinks, as bells malfunction. She knocks. Still no one. Maybe they no longer take guests here, or she's come to the wrong place. But as she looks around, she's sure from Jackson's description that this is where he stayed in the '40s and '50s, when he worked on the Punjab dam. She stands back to take in the house that is visible beyond the gate. It is boxy and made of brick, with ropes of green vines falling from the roof. It looks untouched over decades, a house that was once an army barracks, just as Jackson described.

She rings again, then gives the gate another hard knock. At last a man appears, apologises, welcomes her and ushers her through the grounds, past a few outdoor tables to the main house. No one else is around. He shows her into the kitchen and nods towards another man, wearing a Nehru vest over his kurta, with western trousers below. This man will help her, he says. The Nehru-vested man pours tea and places it on the circular table with a white cloth, where he invites her to sit and wait. He tells her he will be back when her room has been prepared. He leaves her alone, and she sips her tea, though she has no real desire for it. She is suddenly extremely tired.

She gets up to fight off her fatigue and begins to stroll around the large kitchen, examining the appliances on the counter. Like the Singer sewing machines in Gaggal, these are antiques, sturdy and thick — a kettle, a dangerous-looking toaster and three ancient samovars perched on a shelf. She imagines Mrs Bhandari here. His hostess, Jackson had told her, stitched clothes for the refugees who arrived in Amritsar during Partition. Reema sees her making meals for them here, too, serving tea in the Victorian china cups, not caring if they broke. 'Mrs Bhandari ran her own show,' Jackson said, hosting men and women from around the world. Reema would like her to appear in the kitchen, so that she could ask her about Jackson as a young person — understand more things about a man from his era — but it's unlikely that the woman is still alive.

She opens a door beside the pantry that leads into a different part of the house. She follows a narrow hallway to another door, pokes her head into what appears to be a sitting room, and then slips into it. She seems to be the only guest here. All is quiet. The walls are lined with bookshelves packed with old books. Mahogany armchairs and a patterned rug form the centre of the room. Photographs are hung from high on long silver chains, and others are stacked up on a coffee table. First she examines the books — *Essays in Biography*, *The Company of Women*, *The Punjab Peasant*, *The Complete Poems of Keats and Shelley*, *Silas Marner*, a tattered copy of *Seven Years in Tibet*. Then she moves to the hanging photos, which seem to be mostly of people, faces that span decades. Shots of a large extended family, then of people who look like visitors, mostly men, young and dishevelled, but a few finely appointed in black jackets and ties, posing with the woman she's sure is the Mrs herself. In one, an English-looking man seems to have his tie secured so tightly, under a collar so high and stiff, that there is no wonder he is frowning beside his hostess in her flowing sari, who is holding up her hand as though to say, *oh go on, hurry up, get this Empire nonsense over with.* In other photos she is older. She wears the expression of one who takes everything with humour, and yet does not suffer fools gladly. A person who recognises that some of her guests have left behind a greater mess in her country than they can fathom, which she and others like her have been forced to clean up.

In another photograph, though, she is laughing, turned to a young white man who smiles as though he's found the secret to life itself. Reema moves closer. The man is dapper, though casually dressed. She's struck by features that she's been staring at these last two weeks. Those ears; the chin is more taut with youth, yes, but surely it's his. She takes this image in. Were they lovers? Is it really him, or is she just wanting it to be Jackson?

She sits down on the tapestry rug and then lies back, sinking under the weight of the last few days. Love is not perfect or singular. Stretching her legs she thinks of what Yosh said about shavasana — you let go of your body and it floats down a river as you watch it from the bank.

A noise startles her and she bolts upright.

'This way,' the man in the Nehru vest says, and she quickly pushes herself up off the carpet and follows him, a journey that takes her outside again, and along an outer corridor of rooms almost like cells, and then past a small stable, where a water buffalo stands tethered to a wooden gate. They reach a courtyard, where the man opens a padlocked door and shows her the room.

'Dhanyavaad,' she says. He nods and leaves.

She slips out of her sandals to stand on the cool concrete floor. In the courtyard there are parrots squawking, and she looks out to catch sight of them. She realises that the courtyard is also a paddock for four water buffalo that gaze up as she opens the screen door. The parrots have gone; the courtyard is quiet. There are three lemon trees in the garden similar to the one at the retreat where wedding guests left their wishes. Soldiers once lived in the sparse cubicle-like rooms that surround this courtyard. Wild parrots and soldiers; there must be sense in this. Are there signs she should look for, the way her mother saw an antelope in Delhi and named her only daughter after it?

When Jackson had described this guest house, his arms had flown up like wings. He continued to talk about his landlady even after the rock was thrown. 'Penniless, semi-clad refugees crossing over to Amritsar,' Jackson had said, his arms in the air. 'She drove back and forth in an open car, back and forth to Lahore.' His arms fell back to his side, as blood oozed from his wound.

The memory of Jackson's voice soothes her. She goes inside and sits on the tiny single bed. She would be fine not ever to leave this room, not to get on a plane, to stay in these barracks and look after the water buffalo. She wonders where Yosh and Monica are now, whether they've reached the snow line and what they might say as they scatter Amelia on the mountain.

She lets herself fall back on the bed. She wants to be an old woman.

She thinks about the distant cousin whose lover ate kuchala, the poison that slowly killed him. What would have happened if he and the cousin had married? She wants someone to love her the way Jackson loved Amelia. No, that is not correct. *She* wants to love someone that way.

Her eyes get heavy, but she needs to go to the bathroom. She forces herself to stand and, when she does, she gets an idea. Retrieving her knapsack, she takes out the notebook and tears out a page. She finds a pen. She thinks hard about Jackson and the right words. Her bladder makes its urgency felt. *I wish for you* … she prints in big, clear letters. What were the best wishes on Jyoti's wishing tree? So many silly ones, rubbish sentiments and corny greeting-card lines. She loses her concentration. *I wish for you* … what? To tell me what happened in the hospital? No, the wish is not for her. For him to be reborn as a woman, labourer, black man? Her bladder presses. To be released from blindness and ambition? She squeezes her legs, trying to shush her bladder. I wish for you *a wish*, she writes quickly. She opens the screen door and hurries outside to the lemon tree. The water buffalo stop chewing to stare at her. She pierces the paper with the tip of a twig on the tree. It rests there. *I wish for you a wish*. She rushes back inside to the toilet.

She sits for a long time, peeing. She takes some toilet paper and wipes herself. Glancing at the paper she sees a reddish-brown stain. She wipes again. The second time there's a bit more and a bit redder. She will not think of that now. It must be nothing.

She lies on the bed. She hasn't set an alarm, but she will wake in time for her flight, the taxi booked, her backpack ready. She will be in London by this time tomorrow. And she will know what's right for her, the way the antelope knew her name.

———

The sky is clear like that New Year's Eve in Brunei, but freezing, and drier than my lips. I stand watching you, Amelia, and there is movement, pirouettes of particles. Phosphate of calcium, incinerated, piled high, ashes upon ashes, the moon is on its side, a lull in the blizzard, the snow has settled, and birds upon birds ... Please, teach me to dance.

Acknowledgements

Many people have shown me their generosity, new ways of seeing, better ways of writing and deeper ways of being; they have shared their stories, offered their skills, given this work their rigour and attention. They are responsible for the existence of this book in many different ways. I hope they will each know how grateful I am for what they have given. Thanks to Divya Kohl, Fides Krucker, Dave Butterworth, Izzy Butterworth, Bella Jackson, Jono Jackson, Raju Ram, Felizitas Fischer, Jakob Urban, Sudarshana, Jeremy Newson, Gina Newson, Stephanie Young, Jennifer Nadel, Marko Jobst, Akshi Singh, China Miéville, Susan Rudy, Sandy Pool, Saba Ahmed, Anjali Joseph; Jackie Kaiser and everyone at Westwood Creative; Molly Slight, Adam Howard, Sarah Braybrooke and everyone at Scribe; Anne Collins, Tonia Addison and everyone at Penguin Random House Canada.

TESSA MCWATT is the author of seven novels and two books for young people. Her fiction has been nominated for the Governor General's Award, the City of Toronto Book Awards, and the OCM Bocas Prize. She is the co-editor, along with Dionne Brand and Rabindranath Maharaj, of *Luminous Ink: Writers on Writing in Canada*, and she won the Eccles British Library Award in 2018 for her memoir: *Shame on Me: An Anatomy of Race and Belonging*, which also won the Bocas Prize for Non-Fiction 2020 and was a finalist for the Hilary Weston Writers' Trust Prize and the Governor General's Literary Award for Nonfiction. She is a librettist, most recently working with British composer Hannah Kendall. Their chamber opera, *The Knife of Dawn*, premiered at the Roundhouse, London, in 2016, and they are working on a new full-length opera. McWatt is the Course Director for the Master's in Prose Fiction at the University of East Anglia and is on the Board of Trustees at Wasafiri. Born in Guyana and raised in Canada, she lives in London.